Is it Warren's imagination. . .or is Kayla at last beginning to respond to his love?

"Oh, Kayla," he whispered and pulled her into his chest. She buried her face in his chest. "Shh, it's going to be okay," he promised.

For the second time in less than a week, he felt Kayla allow herself to open up to him. *Lord, give her strength,* Warren silently prayed.

"I'm sorry. I don't usually fall apart like this." She sniffled and pulled herself from his embrace.

He wanted to pull her back. "You've been under a lot of stress."

"I suppose."

"Kayla, let's sit and talk about what happened today."

"I don't want to talk about Brian."

"Neither do I. I'm referring to the phone message I received, something about Freda." He leaned down and pushed a stray strand of auburn hair from her face.

Kayla looked up at him and searched his eyes, her gaze penetrating deep into his soul. "And we need to talk about us. . .what's happening between us," he said.

LYNN A. COLEMAN is a Martha's Vineyard native who now calls the tropics of Miami, Florida, home. She is a minister's wife who writes to the Lord's glory through the various means of articles, short stories, and a web site. She has three grown children and six grandchildren. She also hosts an inspirational romance writing workshop on the Internet, manages an inspirational romance web site, edits an inspirational romance electronic newsletter, and serves as president of the American Christian Romance Writers organization. Lynn invites you to visit her website http://www.lynncoleman.com.

Books by Lynn A. Coleman

HEARTSONG PRESENTS
HP314—Sea Escape
HP396—A Time to Embrace

Mustering Courage

Lynn A. Coleman

Heartsong Presents

This book is dedicated in loving memory of Freda Irene Blood Putnam, my Gram.

A note from the author:
I love to hear from my readers! You may correspond with me by writing: **Lynn A. Coleman**
Author Relations
PO Box 719
Uhrichsville, OH 44683

ISBN 1-58660-199-7

MUSTERING COURAGE

Scripture taken from the HOLY BIBLE: NEW INTERNATIONAL VERSION®. NIV®. Copyright © 1973, 1978, 1984 by International Bible Society. Used by permission of Zondervan Publishing House.

All of the characters and events in this book are fictitious. Any resemblance to actual persons, living or dead, or to actual events is purely coincidental.

Cover illustration by Kay Salem.

PRINTED IN THE U.S.A.

one

"Kayla!"

Kayla turned off the kitchen faucet and craned her body around the door casing. "Yes, Gram," she yelled, loud enough to wake the dead, though she knew her great-grandmother would barely hear.

"Not you. The other Kayla."

Kayla rolled her eyes, slumped back into the kitchen, dried off her hands, and went to her grandmother. "Hi, Gram."

"Kayla," she smiled. "I was hoping I'd see you today."

She took a seat across from her great-grandmother and noticed an old photo album with black pages in her grandmother's lap.

Freda Brown was ninety-two and in the midstages of Alzheimer's. Kayla, the oldest great-grandchild, had finished college and offered to take care of her until the disease progressed to the necessity of twenty-four-hour care. Reluctantly, the family had agreed. Their concerns had focused on her youth and her need for a life of her own. But in Kayla's heart she just couldn't see taking her great-grandmother out of the only home she'd known for over seventy years, an old farmhouse sitting by a lake. Most of the land was being cultivated by area farmers, and the rent helped with taxes and other expenses.

The pictures, brown and yellowed, some faded from the years, while a few were still clear, were of people and places of which Kayla had no knowledge. She reached for the picture in Freda's blue-veined hand. "Who is this, Gram?"

"Oh, that's your brother."

5

"Your brother?" My brother Jeremy is at college, has red-dish brown hair, and is built like a tree trunk. This person is thin as a rail, has black hair—although it is tough to tell in a black-and-white photograph—and he might fit under Jeremy's wingspread. Okay, Lord, who does she think I am now? "Gram, who am I?"

"Honestly, Joann, I don't understand these silly games you play. You know perfectly well who you are!"

Joann, Gram's younger sister. Gotcha! That means this would be a picture of Freda's brother, either Robert or Richard. Which one? Kayla didn't have a clue. "How old is Robert here?" she guessed.

Freda took the snapshot and examined it more closely. Kayla watched as her grandmother's blue eyes darkened with fear from confusion. Freda's hands trembled as her gaze implored Kayla for the answer. After spending many days and months with her great-grandmother, Kayla knew Gram wouldn't ask. Admitting confusion was to admit having dementia. Holding back her own tears, Kayla brushed the gray curls from her grandmother's face. "It's okay, Gram. It doesn't matter right now. Would you like a cup of coffee?"

"Coffee would be nice. You look familiar. . . Do you know my granddaughter, Kayla?"

"Yes, I do."

"She's a fine young woman, isn't she?" Freda asked as Kayla helped her up from a chair and escorted her to the table.

"She's okay. Gram, would you like a cookie?" Kayla knew her great-grandmother had a sweet tooth, and anything sweet was guaranteed instant success. Often Kayla would have to hide the dessert so her great-grandmother would eat her entire meal first.

Dealing with a patient with Alzheimer's took a lot of patience. But Kayla knew the day was coming when even her perseverance wouldn't be enough. She prayed often that the Lord would take her great-grandmother home to be with Him in heaven, long before she suffered. Some days, Kayla thought the request selfish. Other days, like today, when she saw the frustration and confusion Freda experienced, Kayla felt the prayer was justified.

Broken images and memories in her mind. . .misdirected brain waves. . .that was the best way Kayla could imagine the disease. Oh, sure, she knew it was caused by hardening of the arteries in the brain, that the nerve endings were balling up in places. But in the end it simply came down to being unable to recover memories. Whether they were from two seconds or eighty years ago, it didn't matter, not at this point.

Kayla poured her great-grandmother a cup of coffee and handed her the creamer to pour for herself. Another test of patience. It was easier to do it for her, but she needed to encourage Freda's dignity in any small way she could.

Kayla thanked God for the time spent as a child with her grandmother. She had loved visiting the old house, loved playing on the lake. Gram's house remained a childhood memory as strong and vibrant as the woman herself once was.

Kayla poured a glass of iced tea for herself. All through college she could never get herself to drink coffee. She had tried but found it just too bitter for her taste buds. Now she slumped back into the tall Windsor chair and placed her feet on the leg brace under the table. When she was small, she had played under there, using the support structure as an elaborate apartment for her dolls. Of course, Jeremy felt it was the perfect place for his toy cars. It soon became a contest as to who could slip away and gain possession of one of the many fun spots in the house. She slipped off her shoe and felt the beam with her toes. "Gram, do you remember the time Jeremy carved his name in the table?"

"Your father was livid, embarrassed, mostly. You see, when your daddy was little he carved his name in my nightstand."

"Really?"

"Sure enough. I can show you where. I still look at it from time to time." Freda smiled.

Kayla traced the "J" with her big toe. Her brother had suffered for this infraction; he had his jackknife taken away for a month. He was in Cub Scouts at the time, and Dad had taken a corner off of his "chit" card. If he lost all four corners, he'd have to earn the merit badge over. But now, feeling the carving with her toes, her memory of her brother was vivid and special. *It's a wonder how our mistakes can be turned around,* she mused.

"Eleanor, did I tell you about the time Edwin lost his leg?"

Eleanor was Kayla's mother; Edwin, Kayla's great-grandfather. "Tell me." Kayla smiled and took another sip.

"Ed was fifteen at the time. He and a bunch of his buddies were jumping the train, taking rides here and there. Mostly, they just went to the other end of town and such, but this one time he jumped too late and missed. His leg was crushed and severed by the wheels. But it never slowed the man down. He learned to walk with a wooden leg, and he managed to work hard for his family. He made a mistake and he learned from it. God was gracious and spared his life."

Kayla knew the story, and amazingly enough, she understood the connection Gram had made between Jeremy carving his name in the table and their great-grandfather jumping a train.

"Sin is sin," Freda continued to enlighten. "Your brother, your father, and my husband, all sinned at one time or another. But forgiveness covers our mistakes, and we move on."

"I understand, Gram." Kayla, though still young in comparison to her great-grandmother, was well aware of past sin in her own life.

Gram's strong personality, though sometimes grating, generally yielded to the Holy Spirit. When Kayla was younger, she had thought her great-grandmother was simply the sweet little old "grandma" people typically pictured. Now she was learning some of her grandmother's other sides. Because Alzheimer's stripped away self-control, Kayla frequently witnessed some of those angry outbursts she knew had been part of her great-grandmother's earlier life. Freda had told her on more than one occasion of her temper, now controlled by God's grace. Kayla had once found it hard to believe, having never seen her great-grandmother's anger in action. Now she no longer questioned it.

"Kayla," Freda said as she grasped her hand, "I don't like not remembering, being confused. It's a regular pain in the—"

"I know, Gram," Kayla interrupted her as another side of the disease cropped its ugly head. The lack of self-control affected so many areas. Some patients became sweeter, while others had problems controlling their language; the disease manifested itself in each person so differently. Kayla was discouraged by literature that claimed it was common for family members to develop the disease. Kayla petitioned the Lord one more time: *Please protect me from this disease, Lord*. She shuddered at the thought and vigorously rubbed her bare arms.

"Cold?" Freda asked.

"I'm okay." Kayla got up from the table and carried her glass to the sink.

With dinner in the oven, Kayla went to her room to work on the lesson for her Sunday school class, the parable of the mustard seed. Kayla reread the verses from Matthew 13:31–33:

> *"The kingdom of heaven is like a mustard seed, which*
> *a man took and planted in his field. Though it is the*
> *smallest of all your seeds, yet when it grows, it is the*

largest of garden plants and becomes a tree, so that
the birds of the air come and perch in its branches."

The picturesque parable was one of her favorite passages.
But how could she convey the meaning to children who were
only three to six years old. . .? Kayla slid her chair back and
began to pace. She stopped at her bureau, her jewelry box
catching her attention. It was hand-carved teak, a gift from
Grandpa Max, Freda's son, on her thirteenth birthday. A smile
spread across her face. She caressed the finely carved rosebud
on top of the box. *He sure knew how to work with wood,* she
reflected.

Her memory jogged. When she was little, her mother
had given her a charm bracelet—one charm contained a mustard seed. Kayla pulled out the bottom drawer and rummaged
through. There, she found it. It was well-worn, the gold finish
long since faded. In fact, she had two charms with mustard
seeds, she realized. One was a single seed in a bubble of
glass, the other a small, rectangular gold box with plastic windows filled with the small seeds. "Excellent!"

The stove's buzzer went off, and she hurried back to the
kitchen. As she passed her great-grandmother asleep in her
chair, she thanked the Lord that Freda's hearing was less than
perfect.

Kayla pulled out the roasted chicken, baked potatoes, and
glazed carrots, then placed them on top of the stove.

"Smells great! What's for supper?" a male voice called from
the back door.

two

"Excuse me?"

"You mean to tell me you're not going to feed a starving man?" Warren poised a hand to his chest in feigned desperation.

"Warren, you startled me." Kayla pulled off her oven mitts. Warren Robinson was one of the farmers who rented a portion of Freda's property.

"Sorry, but isn't today Tuesday?"

"Yeah. . ."

"And didn't you ask me to take care of Freda tonight?"

How on earth had she forgotten? "Sure," she responded hastily, "there's plenty for dinner." Of course she'd have to nuke another baked potato, but that would only take a few minutes.

Warren stomped his well-worn work boots on the threshold. He stood fairly tall, with dark brown hair and small brown eyes, but he was skinny as a beanpole. It was a wonder the man could even pick up a bale of hay. Kayla wouldn't have believed it possible if she hadn't seen it last summer. "Thanks for coming over, Warren, I do appreciate it."

"You're welcome, Kayla." Warren peeked into the living room. "How's she doing today?"

"All right, I guess. I was only one of two Kaylas today, besides my great-aunt Joann and my mother."

Warren smiled and wagged his head. "Such a shame. She's always been a spitfire."

"That she was." Kayla grabbed the everyday earthenware dishes from the cupboard.

"Can I help?"

11

"Sure." Kayla piled the dishes in his waiting arms. "Set these on the table while I get the silverware and glasses."

"Yes, Ma'am."

Ma'am! Who was he calling ma'am? Warren probably beat her in age by a couple years. He was a nice enough guy, but he fancied himself too familiar with the family. Kayla bit her lower lip. She'd been over this territory before, and she reminded herself again that Warren had been checking up on Freda for years, giving her far more time than anyone in the family had ever been able to do. *Until now,* she amended.

Kayla wasn't sure what bothered her most about Warren, but something did. He seemed to set her on edge every time he came over. Was it that she was jealous of the time he'd spent with Freda? Or was there something truly not right with the man? He seemed intelligent enough, although she'd never had a conversation with him that didn't revolve around Freda. *Ah, phooey, it doesn't matter.* He was a kind man and obviously cared for her grandmother.

Warren relieved her of the glasses and silverware. "Whatcha thinkin'?" he asked.

"Oh, nothing. Sorry." Kayla's face flamed.

૨૦

Warren set the silverware at each place setting. Whatever Kayla was thinking, she was embarrassed to have been caught. For months, he'd been trying to get her attention. For months, she hadn't noticed him any more than a piece of old furniture in her great-grandmother's home. Granted, when she first arrived nearly ten months ago, he had kept an eye on her to make certain she wasn't after Freda's estate. But the truth of the matter was, Warren now felt sure, Kayla had a pure heart. He saw in her a virtuous woman, fitting the Proverbs thirty-one model more and more each day.

So why isn't she interested in me, Lord? Warren prayed.

He knew he wasn't the knight in shining armor that women dreamed about. But he was honest, hardworking, and he genuinely cared for Freda. And yet that wasn't enough. On the other hand, she had gotten into his pores. Every day he prayed for her, every day he fought excuses to come see her. Often he lost the inner battle.

"Patience, My son."

Warren whipped up his head and turned around. Freda was still asleep.

"Lord?" he asked silently. He was suddenly confident God was encouraging him to have more patience. Oddly enough, the passage came to mind where Jesus told His disciples if they had faith they could move a mountain into the sea. Warren released a pent-up breath. "Okay, I'll wait."

"Wait for what?" Kayla asked.

Warren's heart pounded in his chest. The sensation reminded him of when he was younger and his mom had caught him sneaking candy from her hiding place. "Uh," he stammered, "I'll wait for God's timing to answer a prayer."

"Isn't that the worst? I mean, you've got this thing you're praying for and you're certain God's just taking His sweet time. And it doesn't seem to matter at the moment that He's answered prayers before. You only see the obstacle or the thing you've been praying about," Kayla jabbered on. "Sometimes I wonder if I'll ever be able to fully trust God."

"Guilty," he answered. What else could he say? That the answer to his prayer was standing right there in front of him, yet she didn't have any of the same feelings for him as he had for her?

"I think I ought to wake up Gram."

"Yeah, you know how she likes to eat. I'm surprised she hasn't woken up from the aroma," Warren said.

"I think her sense of smell is shot, too. The other day I

caught her about to eat some potato salad that had turned. The smell was so strong I opened the windows to air out the house. And there she was with a fork ready to dive in."

"Gross." Warren winced.

"You're telling me. I went through the fridge like a wild woman. Threw out everything that might possibly be bad. I'll make sure it doesn't happen again."

"She'd have gotten sick if she had eaten it."

"No kiddin', Cowboy."

Warren shut his mouth quickly. Nope, he didn't need to bait this woman. For some reason, she thought he was ignorant or something. It didn't matter that he'd been to college and graduated in the top of his class. Of course, she'd never asked him about his education; in her mind, he was just some country bumpkin who fell off the turnip truck a mile back or so.

You've got your work cut out for You, Lord. I mean, if she really is the one—and please note I did add the word "if." Was he having second thoughts about Kayla? It was possible. But that's how things went between them. They'd start talking and seemingly be on the same brain wave and boom! She'd throw him a curve. Did he really want to live in the same house with a woman who always had him questioning his own wisdom, or worse yet, made him wonder who he was? Warren pulled out a chair for Freda, slid her and the chair closer to the table, and took the chair to Freda's left. "Evening, Freda, how are you today?"

"Just fine, George. How's your son?" Freda asked.

Warren smiled. She was close: George was his dad. "Son's fine, Freda. Helps me with the farm now."

"You don't say. Wasn't it just yesterday that he started kindergarten?"

"Seems like it." Warren rolled with Freda's conversation. Over the years, her dementia had gotten slowly worse. At first, he had tried to show her the error of her thinking, but that proved useless and only frustrated the woman. On the other hand, sometimes it did get him in a bind when she would remember something. But, by and large, that didn't happen anymore.

Kayla wolfed down her dinner, he noticed, and excused herself from the table. *"Wolfed" might be a bit harsh,* he amended. She was apparently running late. She probably had forgotten all about her meeting this evening.

Meeting? Who was he kidding? It was a date. Brian Jackson had asked her out, pure and simple. It wasn't like Warren could tell her not to go. It wasn't his place. And Brian was a decent enough fellow. So why did the date bother him? *Because I want to be her escort, and I'm jealous,* he admitted.

"So, Freda, what do you want to do tonight?" Warren raised his voice so she could hear.

"Not much for dancing, young man," Freda answered.

"Dancing? How'd she get that out of— Oh, never mind," he mumbled.

Kayla entered the room. " 'Cause she's deaf as a doornail, and you're on the side with her really bad ear."

"Oh." Warren got up and went to Freda's good ear. "Freda, what would you like to do this evening?"

"I'd like to watch the merry-go-round show."

Warren turned to Kayla and mouthed, "What merry-go-round show?"

"That game show that's like hangman."

"Wheel of Fortune?" Warren asked.

"Bingo." He watched Kayla check her makeup in the mirror. Her auburn hair glowed. Her green eyes sparkled. She was happy and excited to be going out with Brian. *Perhaps she isn't the woman for me, after all. Perhaps Brian is the lucky man when it comes to sharing this woman's life.*

He caught her gaze in the mirror. "What?" she asked.

He paused.

"Is there something wrong with my hair or. . .?"

"No, Kayla, everything is fine. You look stunning this evening." Warren turned his back to her. She was beautiful, exquisitely and wonderfully made.

It was time for him to face facts. No matter who he was, he was not good enough for Kayla. She was perfect. He was far less.

Warren walked over to Freda and bent down to her good ear. "Freda, let's set you in front of the television." He slowly eased her to her feet and helped her to her chair. Reaching for the remote, he settled down in a reclining chair across the room from her.

❧

Kayla watched Warren work with Gram. Freda was comfortable with him. Tonight shouldn't be a problem.

Brian had pinned her to finally go out with him. She wasn't all that attracted to the man, but she had run out of excuses. He was handsome enough; she couldn't fault him his looks. But there was no chemistry between them.

She fussed with her hair once more in the mirror. It was odd how Warren's eyes had held hers moments earlier. She snuck another glimpse at him, but his eyes were fixed on the television, his finger on the remote. Kayla grinned. *Typical male.*

A horn beeped in the drive, and Kayla's back stiffened. Her father's words ran quickly through her mind: *"If a boy can't come to the house and greet the parents, he's not good enough to go out with."*

Then the front door rattled in its hinges from Brian's knock. *Phew,* Kayla thought. At least he came to the door.

"Good night, Gram." She kissed Freda on the cheek and opened the door for Brian.

"Ready?" Brian asked. Standing there in his denim jacket and jeans, his broad shoulders and chest drew her eyes.

Kayla guarded her thoughts, not allowing them to go any further. "Ready."

Brian scooped her in his embrace and held her around the waist with his right arm. "Hey, Warren, thanks for watching Freda tonight."

Warren popped his head up from the television. *He seems awfully interested in the game show,* Kayla thought. Warren waved. "No problem, have fun."

Warren's attention moved back to the screen, and Kayla followed Brian's gentle nudge out the door. Outside, he opened the car door for her and closed it. *A perfect gentleman. How nice,* she mused.

She snuggled into the soft leather bucket seats and relaxed. She was due a night of leisure. Gram was fine; Warren would take care of her. This was Kayla's first night off in a very long time. "So, where are we going tonight?"

three

Warren sat on the lakefront that abutted his and Freda's property. Tossing a pebble into the lake, he watched the rings grow larger and larger until they dissolved into the calm of the water. He sighed, weary from lack of sleep, and tossed in another pebble.

Plagued by foolish thoughts of Kayla and Brian, sleep had eluded him. Frustrated with himself, he watched the sun peek its yellow burst of light over the horizon. What did it matter that she hadn't come home until well after midnight? He was acting like the parent of a teenager who had stayed out past curfew.

His stomach knotted at the memory of the words he had spoken to Kayla when she had finally arrived home. Spoken? Spat was more like it. Granted, he had been tired and grumpy. He had only assumed she would be home by eleven.

Kayla hadn't been too pleased with him, either, Warren remembered as he tossed another stone—this one a little larger, and it made a plunking sound as it plummeted below the surface. The first thing he needed to do this morning, besides milking the cows, was apologize. He turned his wrist to look at his watch. Six-fifteen. He scanned Freda's house for signs of life. Nothing moved, no lights were on, not a single sound filtered through the walls. He tapped his hat on his shins and plopped it back on his head. "The cows are waiting, I'll have to come back later," he said to the wind as he worked his stiff body up from the ground.

At home, he discovered his father already in the barn. "Morning, Son."

"Hi, Dad. Sorry."

"Mind telling me what's on your mind?" His father clapped the side of old Betsy and whispered calm and soothing words before he began milking her. The spray of milk pinged into the metal bucket.

Warren shrugged and then leaned against the wooden rails of the pen.

"Kayla?"

"I suppose. I mean, if she wants to date Brian, who am I to say anything?"

"So, she had a date last night?" Another ping hit the bucket.

"Yeah."

"I see." His father continued the milking.

"I know it sounds like I'm jealous, but how can I be when she doesn't even know. . .?"

"Son, why do you care about Kayla? Seems to me you were pretty worked up when she first arrived, believing she was after her great-grandmother's money."

"But that was before I got to know her. She's one of the finest women I've ever seen. I'm not fooling myself—she's got an edge on her that could slice any man in two, but. . ."

"But you got to know her, right?"

Warren nodded his head. He wasn't sure where his father was going with this.

"So wouldn't it make sense to just keep befriending her, letting her get to know you, the real man, just like you've gotten to know her?"

"What about Brian? I can't exactly compete." Warren pushed himself off the rail and started pacing.

"Why not?"

Warren wagged his head. Why couldn't parents see these things? "Because Brian has looks, brains, and money. I don't quite measure up."

"Maybe not."

"There's no maybe about it. I simply can't compete with a man like that."

"No one is asking you to. Warren, would you truly be happy with a woman who fell in love with you for your looks, brains, and money? Or would you prefer a woman who had the same goals as you? Lived for the Lord as you do, laughed at the same kind of jokes?"

"Yeah, yeah, you made your point, Dad."

"Good. Now go take care of the chickens and horses."

"On my way." Warren snagged a bucket of feed and headed to the chicken coop. His dad was right. If Kayla was interested in Brian for all those things, then she wasn't the woman for him—or Brian, for that matter. People needed to be loved for who they were, not for what others thought they should be.

The eggs gathered, the horses fed, Warren washed up and sat down to a good country breakfast. His mother, Ann, was an excellent cook. Weight gain had never been a problem for him. Three eggs, a couple slices of toast, four sausages, juice, and coffee rounded out his meal.

&

Kayla showered after taking care of her grandmother's shower and helping her dress. A simple breakfast of toast with a little jam and coffee was all Freda ate most mornings. Kayla leaned back into the pulsing warm water and worked her fingers through her hair. Her date with Brian had actually been pleasant. Until she arrived home. *Who does Warren think he is, anyway? I'm a grown woman. I can go out and stay out as long as I want.* She poured the shampoo into her hand before working it into her auburn hair.

"I suppose I should have given him a time frame. Frankly, I didn't think it mattered, Lord," she prayed out loud, washing her hair vigorously. She had far too much shampoo for this short new haircut. The lather was getting thicker with each stroke. Scooping off the excess, she continued to massage her scalp.

"Next time I'll let him know," she determined. "Of course, he might be mad enough that he won't ever want to watch Freda again." Kayla worried her lower lip, her hands frozen on top of her head. Was it possible she had jeopardized her only free baby-sitter for Freda? "Oh, please, Lord, help him understand. I promise, I'll apologize, and from this point forward I'll give him a time and keep to it."

Kayla rinsed the suds from her hair and finished her shower. Maybe a peace offering would be in order. *I could make a batch of chocolate chip cookies. Besides, I'd be doing it for Gram, also,* she tried to convince herself. Who was she trying to kid? He was the only baby-sitter she had whom she trusted. *People say that the way to a man's heart is through his stomach.*

Of course, she wasn't after his heart, just his forgiveness and a workable understanding. It wasn't like she was fixing him a candlelight dinner, just a simple batch of cookies. He wouldn't mistake her intentions for something else, would he?

Warren had never said anything, never approached her as if he were interested in her. Not that she would want Warren to be interested in her—just that she was never really sure what he wanted or why he stared at her so often. On the other hand, men did tend to stare at her from time to time; why should Warren be any different? Kayla vigorously dried herself off. The mind was a funny thing. She had no interest in Warren romantically, but today for some silly reason she was contemplating these absurd thoughts.

After getting dressed and making sure Freda was okay, Kayla went out to the backyard where in years past her grandmother had kept a garden. When Kayla had first arrived, she found the yard overgrown and the rock walls falling apart. Slowly, she had been rebuilding it. Often, on warm days, she would escort Freda outside to sit and watch her work. Sometimes Freda's memories would resurface, and she'd mention some of the flowers and herbs she had planted here and there. Now, Kayla scooped a small bucket of topsoil to bring to church for planting mustard seeds.

She had settled on planting the seeds and letting the children watch how quickly the plants would grow. It would be a good object lesson, and one she could point out from week to week. Setting the bucket inside the mudroom next to the back door, Kayla went inside to the kitchen to clean up and begin making her peace offering. She needed Warren. Having experienced a break last night, she realized just how good an evening off was. If she was going to continue living with Freda as the Alzheimer's progressed, she would need more times off. If not. . . She shuddered at the thought and went right to work.

ﾊ

"Smells great!"

Kayla jumped about a foot off the floor. "Warren! You've got to stop sneaking up on me like that." She pushed stray wisps of auburn hair from her face.

Warren smiled. Unknown to Kayla, she had left a trail of flour across her cheek. "Sorry. I generally walk over. Don't suppose that makes much noise in the approach. I reckon I could whistle or something when I enter your backyard."

Kayla smiled, then bit her lower lip.

Goodness, Lord, this woman is going to drive me crazy. Warren silently groaned. *Give me strength.* "I came to apologize for last night."

"I should be the one apologizing. I should have given you a time when I'd be coming home," Kayla offered.

"Forgiven?" he asked.

"Yes. Am I?"

"Without a doubt." Warren winked and looked toward the living room. "How's she doing today?"

"Fine. She's a little sluggish, but other than that she's fine."

"May I?" He pointed toward Freda.

"Of course. You're always welcome, Warren."

"Thanks. After last night I wasn't so sure. . ."

Kayla interrupted. "Forgiven, remember?" She smiled.

Warren had to force his hands from reaching out and touching her. *Why does she affect me so?* he wondered and slipped away to the safety of the living room.

"Good morning, Freda. How are you today?" He bent down and placed a kiss on her soft, wrinkled cheek.

"My, you're handsome this morning."

Warren blushed. "Thank you. So how's my favorite girl?"

"Bones are a bit stiff this morning. Other than that, I'm fit as a fiddle."

"Wonderful."

"How's Mable?"

Mable? Who is Mable? Warren raced through his memories of everyone he knew that was associated with Freda, but came up blank. Tentatively, he answered, "Fine."

"I wasn't so sure that cow would pull through, Ed."

Cow! Ed! Okay, must have been an old cow she and her husband had on the farm one year. "Well, she surprised all of us." That was the truth: He was surprised to find out Mable was a cow. Warren grinned.

❧

Kayla listened from the kitchen with affection. *Warren is so good with Gram,* she admitted. Brian hadn't even spoken with Gram last night, not even a simple greeting of hello. *Strange,* she thought.

She wiped her hands on her apron and wrapped some cookies in plastic wrap. Even though they had both apologized, she still wanted to give Warren the cookies. *Can't hurt to sweeten him up.* After all, Brian had asked her out again this coming Friday night.

Warren kissed Freda good-bye and patted her hand. *He's so gentle with her,* Kayla mused. "Warren?"

"What's up?"

"I–I wanted to give you a little something to thank you for watching Gram."

"Bribing me?" His right eyebrow raised a fraction.

"No, well, not really. It was going to be a peace offering." *He has me nailed. How can he do that so well?*

"Oh. Well, I won't turn down homemade cookies. Thanks." Warren started to head for the back door.

"Warren." Kayla stepped toward him, not wanting him to leave before. . . Suddenly, her foot caught on the old cracked linoleum. Her balance lost, she felt herself tumbling to the floor. Mere moments before her head hit, she found her sprawled body cradled in Warren's strong arms.

"You okay?"

Goodness! She felt so warm and secure in his arms. Her eyes explored his deep brown ones. They reminded her of chocolate, semisweet. She followed his lead as he helped her back to her feet.

His warm callused thumb caressed her cheek.

Stop! Wait a minute, this is crazy. Kayla bolted out of his arms and straightened her ruffled clothing. "Thanks," she mumbled.

Warren held up his thumb. "Flour, it was on your cheek."

"Oh." Kayla blushed. He wasn't making a pass, just simply being a gentleman, again. Kayla wasn't sure if she was more upset that he *hadn't* been making a pass at her. This was crazy.

She needed to get a grip.

Warren crouched on the floor. "This is dangerous, Kayla. Freda could fall and do some serious damage. Old folks break hips real easy, you know."

"I know. I've been waiting on my dad to come by and help lay down a new floor."

"When's he coming?"

"I haven't a clue." She really didn't know. Her dad was a busy man, and Kayla was beginning to get the impression he was a little too busy.

"Tell you what. I have some free time this weekend. What if I give you a hand?" Warren got up and wiped his hands together.

"Would you?"

"I wouldn't offer if I didn't mean it. I'd hate to see Freda fall."

"Me, too. Oh, Warren, that would be wonderful. I'll take Gram to town today and order the materials. How big a piece of linoleum do I need?"

"I'll bring a tape measure around later and measure it out for you."

"Thanks, I appreciate it."

"No problem. I'd do anything for Freda."

Freda. He'd do it for her grandmother, not for her. *So why do I suddenly feel so slighted?*

four

Shortly after lunch, Warren arrived with a tape measure in hand. Kayla had to laugh when she heard him whistle upon his approach to the house. Remembering that now, she smiled as she drove Freda to town. As they left the dirt path of Freda's driveway, the tires scrambled onto the pavement, leaving a trail of kicked-up gravel. "Where are we going?" Freda asked.

"To the store. I thought we'd pick up some new flooring for the kitchen."

"Ed and I bought that years ago. Don't know why we need a new one."

"It's cracked and peeling, Gram."

"Oh. I reckon that's a good reason. What color?"

"I don't know. What's your favorite color, Gram?"

"I've always liked blue. Could we paint the ceiling blue?"

"Not today. Do you want a blue floor?"

"Not especially."

Kayla wasn't sure what she was going to do now. It was possible Gram would forget before they got to the store. But a blue floor wouldn't match the kitchen. Hopefully, she could convince her of a more neutral color, perhaps imitation brick. That would fit the country feel of the kitchen, with its hard-wood counters and knotty pine, clear-varnished cupboards. Then again, it would depend on what was available. She didn't want to turn down Warren's offer to help. There was no telling when her father would come around to lend a hand. And to be fair to her father, his business had kept him very busy this past year. Kayla wondered if she was just getting too focused on

Freda and not enough on life around her.

At Brian Jackson's building supply store, Kayla parked in the handicapped parking space. She couldn't leave her great-grandmother at the doorway to the store and park, and yet she didn't have the sticker for her car yet. The last time she had taken Freda to the doctor's, Kayla had applied for it, but it hadn't arrived.

Kayla opened the door for her grandmother and unfastened the seat belt for her. She stood back and gave her hand to Freda to grasp. Slowly, the frail woman eased her body out of the car. Kayla tightened her grip and scooped her arm around her grandmother's waist. Freda straightened her body and clasped her purse to her side. Kayla smiled and gave Freda her elbow to hold on to as they made their way to the front doors.

Once inside, the mixture of sawdust and metal assaulted Kayla's nose. *Definitely a man's store,* she mused. The flooring department was past the electrical section. Seeing the distance, Kayla realized she needed her great-grandmother's wheelchair, which was in the trunk.

"Hi." Brian smiled.

Kayla could feel her face light up. "Oh, Brian, I didn't think the flooring section was so far back. I need to get Gram's wheelchair. Would you mind staying with her?"

"No, but why don't I get the wheelchair and you stay with her," Brian offered.

"Thanks." Kayla handed him the keys, and he stepped back and turned down the aisle.

"Who was that?" Freda asked.

"His name is Brian Jackson. He's the manager of this store."

"Oh." Freda looked around.

Kayla wasn't sure what was going on inside Freda's mind. Brian reappeared quickly, pushing the wheelchair. "Here you go, Kayla. You really ought to get a handicapped sticker for your car. You wouldn't want to have it towed away."

Kayla eased her grandmother into the chair. "Should have it soon. We already applied for it." She squatted in front of Freda, gently placing her feet on the foot braces. *Odd, how Brian is looking around, not even holding the chair,* she thought.

"So what brings you to my store today?" Brian asked.

"Flooring. I'm going to lay a new floor in the kitchen."

"That's a big project; sure you can handle it?"

Kayla stood up and walked around to the back of the wheelchair. "Warren Robinson is offering to help. Are you busy on Saturday?"

"Sorry, but Saturday is the end of the month. Lots of paperwork."

Kayla wasn't sure why she even asked. She knew he would be busy; but if he were free, she was certain an extra pair of hands would help. "I understand. Well, I better get moving. Don't want to keep Gram out too long."

"Why didn't you just leave her at the farm? You and I could have gone to dinner or something."

"Because she needs someone with her all the time now."

"Kayla, you need to put her in a home. They have places to take care of people like this." Brian pointed to the slumped form of Freda.

Kayla felt her face flush with anger. "She doesn't need to go into a home if she has me."

Brian raised his hands in surrender. "Hey, I was merely making a suggestion."

"Sorry. I hear it too often. People today just think of older folks as disposable."

An employee walked up to Brian and asked for assistance. It was the perfect distraction. Obviously, he didn't think much of caring for the elderly one-on-one. Kayla took a deep breath and slowly exhaled. She pushed the wheelchair forward and made her way to the back of the store. By the time they arrived at the flooring department, Freda was sound asleep. Kayla reached for a lap blanket she kept in the back pouch of the chair and lovingly placed it over her great-grandmother's lap.

She turned and faced the giant array of floor covering. With Gram asleep, she would definitely be saving time in the decision-making process. Kayla grinned and thanked the Lord for small favors.

2a.

Warren savored the last of Kayla's cookies. *That woman can cook.* He grinned and wiped the inside brim of his cowboy hat. *Cowboy.* He tossed his head from side to side. He was as far from being a cowboy as his father was from being an electrical engineer. But the hat was good for shelter from the sun and rain. Not to mention, Warren enjoyed how it looked.

He placed the red handkerchief in his back pocket and the hat on his head. The sun was lowering, and its warmth still filled the air. Summer was only days away. The crops were all planted on his and Freda's property; now he headed out to repair the southern fence.

During the winter, some kids had taken down a section of the fence so they could cross the land with their snowmobiles. Unfortunately, the fence post broke when they attempted to lower the wires. That section of the farm was used for summer grazing for the few cows the Robinsons kept. With his truck fully loaded, he drove to the southernmost part of his family's property.

Warren set about his work. He liked working alone, the fresh air, and the gentle play of the wind on the grass. The field was ready to feed the animals. *Which will in turn feed us,* he mused. *God, You really are quite creative.*

In the distance, he saw a young man approaching. Warren continued to pull out his tools from the bed of the truck.

"Hey, Warren, sorry about the post." Young Tim Daniels walked up, his overgrown blond curls bouncing around his ears.

Warren set down his tools. "Don't you think it would have been nice to tell us when it happened?"

"Yeah, I suppose. I heard you were going to come mend the fence, so I thought I ought to come give you a hand."

"I appreciate the offer, Tim. Put on those work gloves and grab that hunk of barbed wire over there."

"Sure." Tim wriggled on the gloves and helped with the fence wiring almost immediately. *He's not a bad kid, just a bit impulsive,* Warren reminded himself.

"So what are your plans this summer?" Warren asked.

"Not much; helping with the farm when I hafta."

"You don't care for farming?"

"Not much. Every year it's the same thing, and the money stinks."

"True, you won't get rich farming." Warren secured the last bit of wire to the new post. "What do you like?"

"Computers. But Mom and Dad can't afford a new one, and the one we've got is sooo slow."

Warren chuckled. "So why don't you get a job and earn the money for a new computer? They don't cost that much right now."

"I'd have to work forever," Tim whined.

"Perhaps, but wouldn't it be worth it?"

"Maybe. Hey, Warren, when did you get so smart?"

Warren held back a chuckle. "Oh, I think it was this past winter."

"Really? What happened?"

"Nothing, just opened my eyes up a bit. Take Kayla Brown, for example. She went to college, graduated, and what does she do? She comes to live with her grandmother to take care of her."

Tim scratched his head. "I don't get it."

"She gave up her life to help another. In other words, she put aside her career to help Freda."

"But she'll get paid. She'll probably end up with the old Browns' farm."

"Maybe, but I don't think so."

"Why not?"

"Because Freda has other children, and grandchildren, and great-grandchildren. But Kayla is the only one who put her life on hold for her great-grandmother. Says something about a person, don't you think?"

"Yeah, she's loony. You gotta watch out for number one, just like my pa says."

"I beg to differ with your dad on that, but he's not here to defend himself. Let me just say that I think there is more to life than just getting rich or watching out for only myself."

"Are you watching out for your parents, too? They're getting mighty old, you know."

His parents, old? They were in their early fifties, plenty of years ahead of them. But then Tim was maybe all of fourteen years. It wasn't that many years ago when he thought the same. "Ancient" was how he put it one time when he hadn't seen eye-to-eye with his father. Warren chuckled. "My folks have a good many working years left in them. But yeah, I'm watching over them, helping them out. Trying to implement some of the things I learned in college with regard to agriculture and marketing. Take this field, for example. I've let it lay for a couple years now. Put the cattle here during the summer. Next year, I'll be planting this section. Should have a really rich soil. So while the land looks like it wasn't doing anything, it was actually regaining its strength to be fruitful again."

"I know about rotating crops. Pa taught me about that. But I don't recall him putting cows in the field to fertilize it."

"It's a long process, but I think it'll pay off in the end. I could have planted this year, but I wanted it to lay for one more."

"Do you think I could earn enough for my own computer?"

"Sure, why couldn't you?" Warren placed his hand on Tim's shoulder. "Odd jobs are all over the place. Ask around, I'm sure you can find some jobs."

Tim smiled. "You got one?"

"Hmm, I'll have to think about it. But I might be able to come up with something. Will you work hard?"

"Yes, Sir." Tim's stoic stance took on an air of serious commitment.

five

Gram went to bed early after her excursion. Taking her out on special outings seemed to wear Freda out quickly. Kayla reached for the phone and called Warren.

"Hello, Mrs. Robinson, this is Kayla Brown. Is Warren there?"

"Yes, but he's just retired for the evening."

"Oh." Kayla glanced up at the clock. It was only eight. Staying out to midnight must have really put the man out past his normal bedtime. "I'm sorry. Perhaps I could give you a message for him."

"Sure."

"Thanks. Would you tell him I ordered the linoleum, and Brian said he'd have it delivered by Friday? Also, I'm wondering if he might be free to sit with Freda Friday night."

"I'll let him know you called." Ann Robinson's voice sounded tight. "Have a good night, Kayla."

"Good night." The click of the phone ended as "night" passed her lips. Were the Robinsons upset with her also because of last night? Did they think she was just taking advantage of Warren's giving nature? "Oh, I hope not, Lord. I don't want to take advantage of Warren. He's so good with Gram."

She placed the receiver back in its cradle, and the phone instantly rang. "Hello?"

"Hi, Kayla, it's Warren."

"Warren?"

"Sorry I wasn't there to take your call. My mom just gave me the message."

That was prompt. "She said you'd gone down for the night."

"I had, but I got up to get my Bible out of the living room. I just didn't feel I could go to sleep without spending a little time in God's Word."

Kayla grinned in relief. "I know what you mean. There are days when I hit the floor running just taking care of Gram, and by the time I'm lying in bed I realize I didn't take time for the Lord."

"Exactly." Warren cleared his throat. "Concerning Friday night, no problem. But I have a question for you as well."

"Shoot."

"I was thinking I could remove the old linoleum on Friday night, get the floor ready for the new flooring, and make shorter work of it on Saturday."

"That's fine with me, but I want to help you." Kayla wrapped the phone cord around her finger.

"That's the other thing I wanted to ask you about."

What on earth is the man talking about?

"I met up with a teen today, Tim Daniels, and it seems the boy might be needing some odd jobs to help buy a new computer. So I was wondering if it'd be all right to bring him with me."

Kayla hadn't been planning on paying anyone, and she had purchased high-quality flooring, figuring there would be no installation charge. "How much will I need to pay him?"

"Sorry, I didn't mean to imply you'd be paying him. I'll pay the boy out of my own pocket. It's just that. . .oh, I don't know, he's at that crossroads in his life where I think a healthy influence might do him some good. Basically, I wanted to know from you if it was okay to bring a stranger into your home."

Warren was hiring the kid just to help influence him? The man definitely went up another notch. "I don't have a problem

I'm sure Gram won't mind the extra company. Should I make dinner for three?"

"Nah, I'm not sure Freda can handle seeing the amount of food a teenager can consume." She heard the laughter in his voice.

He's so easy to talk to, Kayla mused.

"I'll have Tim come over around eight. Freda will be down for the night by then."

"Okay. I don't mind paying Tim." Kayla bit her lip, hoping the pay wouldn't be too high.

"Nope, this is my project. I'll take care of it."

"Okay, if you insist."

"Spent a little more on the flooring, huh?" Warren teased.

"How'd you know?"

"Because it's what I would have done. Good quality materials pay off in the long run."

"Yeah, that's what I was thinking, but I don't know if the family will agree. I mean, it's not like any of them want to come and live on the farm. I imagine they're just going to sell the place when the time comes."

"Kayla, let them know I'd like first ops on buying Freda's farm. It's good land, and your great-grandfather cared for it well. Besides, it's close to my family farm and I'd be able to run both when the time comes."

"I'll let them know. But I seriously don't like talking about when Freda dies." Kayla paced, stretching the phone cord to its limit.

"I know, and I don't either. But I'm hoping to have enough saved so when the time is right I can make your family a good offer."

"I understand, Warren, and I think Gram would like it if the place continued to be a farm, not some subdivision of houses."

"Has a contractor already contacted you?"

Kayla walked back to the small table where the phone was kept. "Actually, Brian brought it up the other night. He sees the property as a great investment, especially with the lake."

"I see. Well, I probably can't compete with a contractor's offer, but I'll make a fair one for a farm."

"I'll let the family know, and I'm sure your offer will be fair."

"Good night, Kayla."

"Night, Warren." Kayla placed the phone back in the cradle and scanned the kitchen floor. To the left of the back door stood a three-tier shelf with boots, gloves, and hats. It wasn't fancy, just something her grandpa Max had built when he was a teen, the dark stain on white pine nicked with years of use. This, and several other items, could be moved to make Warren's job easier on Friday night.

She hated to move anything around in the house. Items out of place played tricks on her grandmother's mind. Freda had enough trouble trying to keep things straight, and Kayla figured she didn't need to add to it.

I'll move the items during Gram's nap on Friday afternoon, and I'll still have time to get ready for my date with Brian. Her time with him the other night had been pleasant enough, although he tended to speak about himself more than express any interest in getting to know her. Maybe she was just looking for too much—a hero, the knight on the white horse, who would love her enough to devote himself to her and her only.

Kayla let out a deep sigh and clicked off the kitchen light. Shutting down the house for the night, she made her way to her bedroom.

"Okay, Lord, he can devote himself to You, too, and any children we might have, but I can't cotton to any man so. . .so. . .I don't know. . .in love with himself that he has no appreciation for anyone else." Kayla flipped open her Bible and looked over the lesson of the mustard seed again.

"You know, Lord. I always thought this passage was about faith, 'if you have the faith of a mustard seed.' But here in Matthew it's talking about the kingdom of heaven."

Kayla flipped to the back of her Bible and looked up the word *mustard*. Sure enough, there was another passage where the Lord used an illustration of the mustard seed. In fact, there were five verses that had the word mustard in it. Two were about faith, and three were a comparison with the kingdom of heaven.

Obviously, her lesson about the mustard seed for the children would require more study. She certainly wouldn't allow herself to teach something wrong to impressionable children.

❧

Warren closed his Bible and knelt beside his bed. "Lord, I knew You had a reason for Tim Daniels and myself getting together today. If I can help him see Your truth, allow Tim to come and work with me Friday night. But if I'm trying to do something in my own strength and You've not ordained it, allow him to be busy or even uninterested. And, Lord, thank You for Kayla's willingness to allow Tim into Freda's home. I know how hard it is on Freda to have strangers, so please try and ease her mind.

"You know my heart concerning Freda, so I won't pester You again. She's special, Lord. She always had a kind word and a way of getting me to see things clearly. I reckon that's part of her bluntness, but it is hard to see someone who loved and served You for so many years lose her self-control." Warren chuckled. "I don't think I've heard so many swear words since I was in high school. But I know it's not her, just the damage of this horrible disease."

He got up from his knees and pulled down the sheets. "Oh, and Lord, about Kayla, are You sure? I mean, am I reading

You correctly that she's the one You've designed for me?" He slipped under the covers and rolled to his side.

"Although there was that moment," he mumbled into his pillow, "when I had her in my arms. If I didn't know better, she almost looked like she enjoyed being there. That is, until she realized it was my arms. Oh, Father, if I only could muster the courage to ask her."

Warren clicked off the nightstand lamp, snuggled the blanket over his shoulder, and held it to his chest. "I know she's not ready, Lord, but how long must a man wait?"

With the question on his lips, exhaustion from the lack of sleep the previous night swept over him. All the questions and concerns he had prayed over the night before were still left unanswered. Perhaps his dad was right. Perhaps Kayla just needed some time to get to know him.

Warren yawned and snuggled his head deeper into his pillow. "Tomorrow I'll think about this. Tomorrow. . ." His words trailed off as sleep overtook him.

❧

At the cock's early morning crow, Warren pulled the pillow over his ears and moaned. The cock crowed again. Warren tossed the pillow to the foot of his bed and plopped his feet on the floor.

The farm and early morning chores demanded his attention. Pulling on a pair of denim jeans and a flannel shirt, he slipped his feet into an old pair of boots. He worked his way down the hall and heard his father's footfalls.

"Go back to bed, Dad. I'll take care of everything this morning."

"Thanks, Son," his dad mumbled behind the closed door, and Warren heard the bedsprings creak.

Downstairs, he poured himself a cup of coffee in an old earthen mug. He tapped the automatic coffee machine. "Thank

You, Lord, for modern technology," he muttered gratefully and headed for the barn.

The ever faithful cock crowed again. " 'Mornin', Ralph," he called out to the proud bird.

Ralph flew down from his post and followed Warren the rest of the way into the barn. Ralph was getting on in years. Warren had raised him from an egg as his first 4-H project. Warren had actually won first place that year, not so much because he raised the bird successfully, but because he kept a thorough journal of Ralph's progress.

Warren tossed a handful of corn over to Ralph and proceeded to take care of the rest of the animals. A grain farm didn't need cows and chickens, but the Robinsons always had a few on hand and used them to take care of the family's needs. There were days when Warren wished they bought groceries like everyone else. But most days he saw the logic of being self-sufficient. Too many times, tax bills strained the total profit for the season.

Ralph continued to follow Warren along his morning chores. The rooster in some ways had become like a pet dog, although Ralph wasn't very fond of dogs. He preferred to perch on the railings and flap his wings at the nosy beasts. Warren chuckled. Sixteen years was getting on in bird years, though Ralph didn't show any signs of getting old.

As he approached the chicken coop, he turned and ordered the rooster, "Stay, Ralph."

The bird stopped in his tracks, but when Warren turned to walk toward the chicken coop again, out of the corner of his eye he saw Ralph take a step forward.

"Ralph, behave yourself."

The bird paused again.

"Good boy."

Ralph flapped his wings and puffed out his chest. Warren

tossed his head from side to side.

Warren collected the eggs, and Ralph flew up, walking the rail beside him. "You know, Ralph, life on a farm is pretty uneventful."

❧

"Hello?" Kayla answered, pulling the receiver to her ear.

"Kayla, it's me, Brian."

"Hi, what's up?" Kayla glanced at Freda sleeping in her chair.

"I was wonderin' if you thought any more about selling the place?"

"No, it's like I said, Brian. It's not mine to sell."

"Yeah, I know, but you're in charge now. Your great-grandmother certainly can't think for herself."

Kayla's back stiffened. Brian's words were true enough, but for some reason they bothered her. "No, I've not thought about it. Why do you ask?"

"A gentleman was just in my store, a local contractor, and he was talking about some really exciting plans for our town. I think you ought to talk with him, Kayla. It could mean so much for our community."

"I don't know."

"Come on, what could it hurt?"

Hurt? Nothing, probably. But she didn't want to be in this position. Her grandmother wasn't dead, so why should she even consider selling the property at this time?

"I'll get back with you about it, Brian. I'll need to talk with my family, Freda's family."

"Fair enough. But seriously, Kayla, it's an excellent plan."

six

"Hi, Dad, I need to talk. Give me a call." Kayla hung up the phone after leaving the brief message. What was the family going to do? No one wanted to be a farmer, and yet she knew Freda desired to have the land remain in the family and to continue to be farmed.

"But we're not farmers, Lord," Kayla petitioned. "And what about Warren Robinson? He wants the land, too. But Brian says the entire town would benefit from the selling of the land to this contractor."

Kayla tried to imagine the small farmhouse as a row of town houses surrounding the lake. Across the lake, there were already town houses where one farm had sold out to a local contractor. They seemed handsome enough for town houses, she supposed; but, on the other hand, they didn't seem to fit with the rolling farm landscape.

Kayla placed a loving hand on top of her grandmother's. "Hi, Gram."

Freda's eyes snapped open, and her body jerked.

"Sorry, Gram, I didn't mean to startle you." Kayla knelt down beside her. "I thought you might like to go outside and help me with the garden."

A smile creased Freda's face.

Kayla helped her up and escorted her slowly out the back door to the patio garden. She fetched a tall glass of iced tea for herself and Freda and sat down beside her.

"Gram, have you ever thought about selling this place?"

"Oh, sure, many times." Freda sipped her tea.

"Why haven't you?"

"Ed wanted to keep the land in the family."

Kayla watched her grandmother. There were moments like these when she was completely lucid, and yet Kayla knew these moments were scattered and could be lost in the blink of an eye.

"But no one wants to farm the land." Kayla prayed she wasn't pushing her grandmother.

"True, money is better elsewhere. But there's something about the dirt between your fingers that gives one a real appreciation of Scripture."

Kayla scanned her memory and couldn't recall a passage that spoke of the dirt between one's fingers. However, the passage of the mustard seed certainly fit with farming. And zillions of other Scriptures related to farming, sowing, and seeds.

"Gram, do you recall the verse in Scripture that talks about the kingdom of heaven being like a mustard seed?"

"Sure do. Down by the lake you'll find one."

The lake? Had Gram already slipped back into the confused recesses of her mind? "A mustard seed?"

"For goodness sakes, Child, of course not. Those are itty-bitty seeds. There's a mustard plant, a good-size scrub now. Just like the Bible says, the birds of the air can build a nest in it."

Had her grandmother taken the illustration of a mustard seed and planted a mustard seed down by the lake years ago?

"A delicate yellow flower," Freda rambled on. "Used to gather the seeds to make my own mustard."

"Really?"

"And catnip, too."

Catnip? *Okay, she's definitely slipped now,* Kayla realized. But was there a tree down by the lake? How could she recognize it?

"Kayla, are you going to have a baby?" Freda asked.

"No." Kayla's cheeks flamed. "I'm not married."

"Oh. Well, why not?"

"Haven't found the right man yet," Kayla explained.

Freda put down her glass of iced tea and pushed herself up out of her chair and wandered over to the left wall of the garden. "See these." Freda pointed to a patch of lovely purple violets.

"Yes."

"Ed planted those for me when we were first expecting Glenn."

Kayla grinned at the annual flower that continued to renew itself from year to year.

"See those daffodils?"

Kayla followed Freda's shaking finger to a crop of daffodils.

"Those were his gift for the birth of Max."

"They're wonderful reminders." Kayla wrapped one arm around her great-grandmother. She worried about Freda's ability to remain steady on her feet.

"At one time, there were plants for all my children, grand-children, and great-grandchildren. This farm represents our family. I could never sell, not even for the million dollars that was offered."

"Million dollars?"

Freda's eyes darted back and forth, scanning Kayla's face.

"Yep. But I wouldn't sell, and I fixed it so they can't buy the land."

"What?" Kayla struggled to calm her voice. "Gram, what are you talking about?"

"Robert never understood the value of money."

Robert? Freda's older brother, Robert, was long dead. What did he have to do with the value of the farm? Had there been a time in the past when the farm was worth a million dollars? Granted, 500 acres was a fair amount of land, but when would it ever have been worth a million dollars? Was it worth that today? Goodness, Kayla prayed her father would call soon.

❧

"Hey, Warren, thanks for watching Freda the other night." Brian extended his hand to him.

Warren accepted it but wondered who Brian had brought with him and why he'd come out to the farm.

"Warren, this is Mack Jefferies. He's looking into purchasing some land. In particular, he was wondering if you might be interested in selling."

Warren accepted Mack's hand. He was a ruggedly built man, obviously unafraid of hard work but dressed in a business suit, his dark hair slicked back. Warren wondered if he was about to get a used-car-salesman approach.

"Sorry, land isn't for sale."

Mack cleared his throat. "I can see you run a nice farm. Makes a profit, I imagine."

"Yes, Sir."

Brian took a step back.

"I'm not here to force you, Warren. I'd just like to give you something to think about. Brian, here, says your family owns 500 or so acres."

Warren nodded.

"He also says your property abuts a third of the lake."

Warren nodded again.

"Would you be interested in selling, say, 50 acres around the lake, with an access road to the lakefront property?"

"I doubt it. The lake feeds the farm."

"Hmm, well. Maybe we can work something out. Would you mind giving me some of your time to discuss the matter?"

"Mr. Jefferies, I'm sure you'd make a fair offer, but I'm seriously not interested in selling the land. The farm is necessary to feed the community."

"Housing and taxes would help this community. New jobs, stores. . .all kinds of businesses would spring up."

"I imagine they would, but I'm not interested."

Brian coughed. "Is the decision yours to make, Warren?"

Mack eyed him. Warren studied Brian. What was he up to? "Nope. Fact is, the land still belongs to my father for a few more years."

"May I speak with him?" Mack asked.

"He's in the barn. Brian will show you the way." Warren turned away, the iron blade back on his shoulder. He had to repair the plow.

It didn't take Brian and Mack long to make their exit from the barn. Warren knew his father wouldn't be interested in selling, but the grin on Mack's face gave him pause to be concerned.

"See you, Warren," Brian called as he slipped into Mack's shiny new pickup truck.

Something was up. And the fact that Brian had brought up selling Freda's property to Kayla made him even more concerned. Was Brian simply using Kayla to get his hands on her property? But what was in it for Brian? Obviously, Mack Jefferies was the man in charge.

Warren pulled off his hat and wiped the sweat from his brow. Nope, something wasn't right. But he didn't have a clue as to what it was.

A few moments later, he saw his father stomp from the barn and over to the house. Warren put down his tools and followed his father.

The kitchen's dim light made him blink several times. "Can you believe it, Ann? The nerve!"

"What?" Warren asked.

"Mack Jefferies. He offered me an incredible amount for the waterfront property. Says I'd be providing for my family better than I have been for years," George huffed.

"Now, George, relax."

"It's not right, Ann, to come on a man's land and insult him." George sat back in his chair.

Warren wondered if Mack Jefferies's insults had brought that grin he'd seen on the man's face.

"Warren, I'm right in assuming you still want this place?"

"Yes, Sir. Nothing has changed."

George gave a curt nod. "Then it's settled. We aren't selling."

Warren grinned, but his smile slipped when he thought of Kayla and whether or not the money would sway her to sell Freda's place to Mack Jefferies. "Dad, how much was he offering?"

George knitted his eyebrows.

"I'm not interested in selling," Warren explained, "but I'm sure he'll be making an offer to Kayla to buy up Freda's place."

"Oh. Well, $500,000 for the whole place and $100,000 for the waterfront property."

Warren let out a slow whistle. "How can Freda's family turn that down?"

George clasped Warren's shoulder. "Trust the Lord, Son. If it's His will for you to buy Freda's property, He'll make a way. Otherwise, it wasn't meant to be."

Warren nodded. He knew his father was right, but all his plans and dreams for expanding the farm rested on buying Freda's place.

&

Surprised by the doorbell, Kayla left her grandmother on the patio and scurried to the front door.

"Brian?" She opened the door. Beside him stood a well-built man in his late forties, maybe early fifties.

"Hi, Kayla. This is Mack Jefferies, the gentleman I told you about who was interested in buying your farm."

Kayla knitted her eyebrows and fired off a silent "you've stepped too far" message to Brian before turning and accepting Mack Jefferies's hand. "Hello, I'm afraid Mr. Jackson has misled you. The property is not for sale."

"I understand the owner is mentally incapable of running the farm." Kayla knew the minute the man spoke she wouldn't trust him. He seemed like the used-car salesman that tried to sell her a lemon when she first went to college; his sales pitch so smooth you almost believed him. However, a bit older and hopefully more experienced, Kayla squared her shoulders and faced this gentleman's plastic smile.

"That's true, but the family, who inherits the property, has decided it is not for sale."

"Ah, I'm sorry to bother you, Miss Brown. Here's my card, and on the back is an offer for the entire estate should the family decide to sell the property."

Kayla took the small white card and turned it. Her eyebrows shot up. Slowly she counted the zeros following the number five—one, two, three, four. . .five. She glanced back at Mack Jefferies and then quickly caught a glance of Brian.

"I told you a contractor would be interested in your property," Brian answered smugly.

"I see, and you would develop town houses on the waterfront, and what, family homes on the rest?" For Brian's sake, she'd hear the man out, but if he ever attempted to sideswipe her again. . . Kayla interrupted her own thoughts. Revenge and getting even were the Lord's job, but sometimes she wanted to get in the mix.

"Actually, I was leaning toward a mall, new school, and, yes, town houses on the lakefront property."

"Are there enough people in Lakeland to fill all those places?" she inquired.

"Not yet, but the city is expanding, and Lakeland will be a perfect bedroom community for those traveling to and from the city." Mack Jefferies seemed to relax his shoulders a bit. *Perhaps he thinks I'm interested.* Not that she had the authority to sell the farm, anyway.

"But it's an hour's drive on the highway to the city." Kayla couldn't believe anyone would drive an hour a day each way to work in the city and commute to the country.

"Times are changing, Miss Brown. Folks work out of their homes with the use of the Internet, faxes, and other technologies. Offices don't mind having employees work at home as long as the work is done."

"I see. Well, I'll pass your offer on to the family, but don't get your hopes up. Gram was pretty adamant about keeping the land in the family."

She wasn't sure how to get rid of these men, and she certainly didn't want to leave Gram alone much longer.

"I understand family traditions. But there comes a time in every man's life when he has to decide what is best for his family and his children over what was best for his parents and their parents before them. It's a generous offer."

Generous? Who is he kidding? Gram just told her she'd been offered a million for the farm. *He's only offering half, and who knows how long ago the million-dollar offer had been made.*

"Kayla?" Freda called from the backyard.

"Excuse me, gentlemen. Gram needs me. Have a good day." Kayla thanked the Lord for Gram calling her. How else did you get away from someone so insistent on trying to change your mind?

seven

The phone rang as she headed toward her grandmother. Kayla grabbed the portable on her way to the patio. "Hello."

"Hi, Honey, what can I do for you?"

"Daddy. It's so good to hear your voice." Kayla released her pent-up breath and escorted her great-grandmother into the house.

"What's wrong?" Charles asked.

"Nothing. Gram's fine. It's just some questions have come up, and I needed to talk with you. Hang on while I get Gram settled in her chair."

"Sure."

Kayla heard her father rustling some papers while she placed the phone down. She helped her great-grandmother settle in her favorite chair and turned on the television. Then she grabbed the phone and headed through the kitchen out the back door, the farthest distance from the television, so she could hear her father.

"Hi, Dad. Sorry."

"No problem. So what's the emergency?"

"The property. I've been getting offers from various sources to buy the land." Kayla turned her back to Freda.

"I see. What kind of offers?"

"Well, Warren Robinson would like to purchase it, but he didn't give a dollar amount; just said it would be a fair price for farmland. Then this contractor came by today and offered $500,000."

"For 500 acres?" her father asked.

"Yep."

"His bid is too low," Charles hissed.

"What?" Kayla couldn't believe Gram's little old farm was even worth the $500,000, let alone a million.

"My father had an offer of a million back twenty years or so. Folks have been wanting that land for years."

"Oh. What should I say?" Kayla turned and faced the lake. Why was there a sudden interest in the property? She had been here for ten months, and all of a sudden she received two offers.

"Tell them it isn't for sale." Her father's office chair creaked in the background. Kayla could see him leaning back and putting his feet on the desk.

"I did, but no one will listen."

"Honey, Gram changed her will a few years back. I don't know what it says. In fact, you should probably be looking for it and any of her other important papers. But she spoke with my sister and me before she wrote it. She was quite concerned with the property remaining in the family and remaining as a farm. I don't know what she decided to do, but I'm certain she's got some clause in there about not selling it to a developer."

"She does have a deep love for this place."

Her dad chuckled. "Yeah, she does. In fact, we all do. It just hasn't been practical to live there and raise our families."

"Why?"

"I guess because our jobs and careers didn't involve growing crops. You know me, Honey. I can't keep a single potted plant alive, never could. I enjoyed working the farm each summer with Gram when I was a boy, but it wasn't the place for me. You're the only one in the family that can grow things well, and your mother, of course."

Kayla leaned against the screen door. "I know, Daddy. It's

just a shame Gram can't have her wish."

"I figure Freda put a clause in the will that will allow us to sell the place after a few years. She wanted it as a place for us to come home to, to enjoy for the summers, vacations, family get-togethers, that sort of thing. Whatever we decide to do with the place won't happen until after Gram has died. So you can tell them we aren't interested."

"All right."

"So, tell me about your date the other night."

"How'd you know about that?"

"Warren told me when I called to check up on you."

"Oh. Well, it was all right."

"Doesn't sound promising." Her father chuckled.

Kayla laughed. "No, I don't suppose it does. The man talked the entire time about himself and selling the farm."

"I see."

"Do you think Warren will want to continue renting the land after Gram's gone?"

"If he can't buy it, I suppose so. Why do you ask?"

"Well, it keeps the place in the black. And as long as it is in the black, it won't be costing us to take care of it."

"True."

"What about inheritance tax?" Kayla walked to the doorway of the living room and peeked at Freda. She was asleep. Kayla clicked the remote.

"That will be the killer. Be nice if Congress would overturn that law. Gram fall asleep again?"

"Yeah. I have to wear earplugs if she watches too much television." Kayla looked down at the linoleum. "Oh, by the way, Warren's coming over this weekend to replace the kitchen floor. Any chance you can come and give a hand?"

"I'd love to, Sweetheart, but I'm going out of town on business this weekend. Let me write a check for Warren."

"Daddy, I think the man would be insulted. He truly loves Gram."

"I reckon so. Okay, what's the cost of the materials? I'll write you a check."

"I paid for it with Gram's household account. Ever since I've taken over the checkbook, she's not buying those foolish sweepstakes offers, thinking she's won a million dollars."

"You're a godsend, Child. I don't know what we'd do without you caring for Gram."

"I love her, Daddy."

"We all do, Sweetheart. But you've put your life on hold for her. That's extraspecial."

"She'd do the same if it was one of us," Kayla responded.

Her father's chair creaked again, signaling it was time to get back to work. "Well, I've got to go, unless there's something else."

"Nope, just concerned about these offers."

"Ignore them. There's nothing we can do about them now, anyway. Look for Gram's will when you get a chance. She used to keep it in her desk."

"Okay. Thanks, Dad."

"You're welcome, Sweetheart. Bye."

Gram's will. Why hadn't she thought to look for it long before now? Kayla placed the phone back in the charger and scurried to Freda's desk.

❧

Warren was pleased that Timothy Daniels would be helping him with Freda's flooring. The boy jumped at the chance to earn some extra money. It seemed his talk with the boy had started him thinking.

The rest of the evening, Warren fought the desire to go and see Kayla. He wrestled with images of her being swayed by Mack Jefferies and Brian to sell the land. It was a tempting offer, he had to admit. And there was no way he could ever come up with that kind of money to make a counteroffer. But his father's words rang over and over again in his head: *Trust in the Lord.*

Warren slapped his Stetson on his knee and headed for the lake. There were a few things he needed to trust God about, and watching the sun slip down past the horizon had always been a wonderful catalyst for a good quiet time. At the lake, he dismounted his horse and looked at the town houses that had sprung up last year, after the Richmonds sold their farm two years prior. He led the horse down to the water's edge for a drink.

Warren scanned the edge of the lake and over to the pier on Freda's property. A small sailboat and rowboat used to sit at that pier. He'd never seen Kayla out on the lake. Of course, when could she go without bringing Freda? *Wouldn't be safe, Lord,* he prayed, agreeing with Kayla's decision. That is, if she had even made a decision regarding the boats.

He found himself walking closer and closer to the abandoned pier. The mustard tree Freda had planted years ago was in full bloom. Bright yellow flowers filled the small tree or large bush. . .it was hard to tell exactly what it was now. Warren chuckled, remembering the season the honeybees found the mustard blossoms. The entire batch of honey had a slight mustard taste. Of course, Freda simply relabeled the bottles and called it honey mustard.

"She was a pip, Lord," Warren chuckled. He missed Freda and the talks they had when he was younger. When he had returned from college, she had begun experiencing some memory problems, but Warren never thought it would develop to the extent it had.

Warren tethered the horse to a tree and sat down on the dock. He remembered Freda explaining the parable of the mustard seed and how that little seed was like our faith. "Yeah, Freda, I'm still learning. I need to trust God and have more faith."

"In what?"

Warren jumped from the dock.

Kayla's bright green eyes danced.

"You scared the living daylights out of me."

Kayla laughed. "Yeah, I noticed. So, what do you need more faith in?"

Warren felt his cheeks burn. "Kinda personal."

"Sorry." Kayla pointed to the bright yellow flowers. "Is that Gram's mustard tree?"

"Yep."

"Wow, it's huge."

"It's been here for quite a while. Speaking of Freda, where is she?"

"In the house, sleeping. I thought I'd come out for a quick peek. She mentioned the mustard tree earlier."

"Oh." Somehow, he was hoping she had seen him and decided to visit. But that would be asking too much. Not to mention, you couldn't see the pier from Freda's home. "So, what kind of conversation with Freda brought up the mustard tree?"

"I did, actually. I'm working on this week's Bible lesson for the kids, and it's driving me crazy. Jesus used the story to explain the kingdom of heaven, and yet that's not the verse people tend to remember about the mustard seed."

"You mean the other one about the faith comparison."

"Right. But my lesson is supposed to be on the parable about the kingdom of heaven. I figure we can plant some mustard seeds and watch them grow."

"That could be a fun project for the kids. Did you know that a mustard seed goes from seed to seed in less than thirty days?"

"Isn't that kind of fast for a seed?"

"One of the fastest. Which, I think, is why Jesus used it in His illustration of the kingdom of heaven."

"Really?" Kayla sat down on the pier beside him.

"Kayla, I'd love to sit and chat with you, but I don't like the idea of Freda being alone for long."

"Oh, my." Kayla jumped up. "I completely forgot." She started toward home. "Would you like to come to the house and finish talking about this with me?"

"Love to, but why don't I take my horse home, and I'll come over after I get him settled in the barn?"

"Okay. See you later." Kayla waved and hurried back to the house. Warren watched her departure with longing, wishing he could run up to her and swoop her in his arms.

Warren jerked his head away and turned to his horse. "Come on, Boy, let's give you a workout on the way home."

❧

Relieved to find Freda still asleep in her chair, Kayla went to the kitchen and washed the dishes before Warren arrived. She hadn't given much thought to the gestation period of a mustard seed. With Warren being a farmer, she guessed he knew these things. But it did put an interesting spin on the parable. If the kingdom of heaven was like a mustard seed growing, and yet it produced new seeds in less than a month. . . *Hmm,* she thought. "Kinda implies that the kingdom of heaven grows and multiplies quickly."

Kayla rinsed her hands and checked on Freda again. She didn't have the heart to wake her, but she didn't want her sleeping all night in her chair.

"Gram," Kayla yelled.

No response.

Kayla moved closer. She was so still. Kayla's heart raced. Was she. . .?

Thank the Lord, her chest was moving up and down with each breath. Kayla released a pent-up breath.

"Gram." She yelled again closer to her better ear.

Freda's eyes fluttered open. "What? Who are you? What are you doing in my house?" Fear and anger darkened Freda's eyes.

"Gram, it's me, Kayla."

"You're not Kayla. Who are you?" Freda demanded.

"Gram, I love you." Kayla bit her inner cheek. Sometimes it was so hard to see her like this.

"Get out of my house," Freda demanded.

Instinctively, Kayla reached out and placed her hand on Freda's arm.

Freda swung at Kayla. "You get out of my house before I call the police!" Freda started to get up from her chair.

Freda had never before lashed out at her like this. "Oh, Lord, what do I do?"

Freda went to the phone. Kayla started to take the phone from her hand, but instead Freda used it to clock her in the eye. *Man, for an old woman you sure have some strength.* Kayla left her and ran to the kitchen for some ice. She could feel her eye beginning to swell.

"What's all the yelling?" Warren asked from the screen door.

"Gram doesn't recognize me."

"Oh, want me to try?" Warren came into the kitchen.

"Sure, can't hurt. She's calling the police." Kayla placed the ice on the swelling.

"Freda!" Warren called as he entered the room.

"Warren, there's a stranger in the house, trying to kill me."

"Freda, sit down. I'll take care of it. Where's Kayla?"

Freda's eyebrows knitted with confusion.

"I'll find her, you sit down." Warren ushered her back to her seat. "Can I get you a cup of tea?"

Freda spat. "Hate the stuff. Coffee, black."

Warren chuckled. "Okay, Freda, I'll get you a cup of coffee."

Kayla leaned against the counter, holding a towel and ice to her head.

"Are you okay?"

Kayla lowered the towel.

"Oh, man. What did she do to you?" He came up close beside her.

"Used the phone as a lethal weapon."

"You're not bleeding," he offered.

"Thanks, Cowboy, I think I could have figured that out on my own." Kayla placed the ice back on her throbbing head.

Warren chuckled. "She got you good." He placed a mug of water into the microwave.

"She's never done this before," Kayla mumbled in disbelief.

"No, but it is common. I'm afraid it means she's slipping further."

"I don't know if I can take these hallucinations. And it's so strange. Today she had a very coherent talk with me. I just don't understand this disease."

"No one does. That's why it's so puzzling." Warren stepped closer. "Let me get a good look at your eye."

A shiver traveled up Kayla's spine.

She lowered the towel.

His breath feathered across her cheek.

Her knees just about buckled when he touched her.

Kayla gulped. *Gram must've hit me harder than I thought.*

eight

A desire to kiss Kayla's cheek rocketed through Warren with such intensity he pulled away. "You're going to have quite a shiner."

"Thanks. Do you think it's safe for me to go in there?" Kayla blinked her green eyes and looked at the floor.

She must be embarrassed to have been hit by Freda. "Yeah, I think she's over it," he tried to reassure her.

Her footsteps faltered as she headed into the living room. Warren placed his arm around her waist to support her. She leaned into him for a moment. Then, gaining her strength, she tentatively inched toward Freda.

"Hi, Gram."

"Kayla." Freda's eyes sparkled with tears. "I was so worried about you."

"I'm fine, Gram."

The microwave signaled. Warren pulled back and fixed Freda a cup of decaffeinated coffee. What Freda didn't know wouldn't hurt her, and this would allow her to sleep tonight.

"Did the bad woman hurt you?" Freda inquired of Kayla. Kayla looked up at Warren, searching his face for an answer. Warren nodded.

"Yes, Gram, but I'm fine."

It wasn't really lying, he told himself. After all, it was the bad woman who controlled Freda when the Alzheimer's reared its ugly head.

"Here's your coffee, Freda. Would you like to sit at the table?"

"All right." Kayla helped her grandmother up from her

58

chair and brought her over to the table.

"Can I get you something?" Warren asked.

"I'm fine, thanks." Kayla sat beside her grandmother and placed the iced cloth over her eye.

"Kayla, I can come back another night."

"No," she said a bit too quickly. Was she worried that Freda might lash out at her again? "I'd really like someone to talk with tonight. If you don't mind."

"No problem."

Warren watched as Freda calmed down and drank her coffee. In mere minutes, she forgot the entire incident. Kayla came up with another story about how she bruised her eye, letting her grandmother off the hook.

He made himself at home, cleaning up the coffee cup and saucer, while Kayla put Freda down for the night.

"She settled?" he asked when Kayla returned to the kitchen.

"For now. That was really strange."

"I can imagine. She just flipped out on you?" Warren tossed the damp dishtowel over his shoulder and returned the cup and saucer to the cabinet.

"Yeah. Thanks, for helping to calm her."

"Anytime. My mom said that when her grandmother developed Alzheimer's, she always seemed more receptive to a man's instructions, rather than hers or her mother's."

"Interesting. I wonder why."

"Don't have a clue. My only guess is that it has to do with male-female chemistry."

"Whatever it is, I'm grateful. I was at a total loss."

Warren reached out and took Kayla's hand. "It may be getting to that time, Kayla."

Tears beaded on her eyelids. She bit her lip. Swallowing hard, she spoke. "I was hoping to at least get through the summer before I had to put her in a home."

Driven by compassion and the desire to comfort, he

embraced Kayla and pulled her to his chest. She wrapped her arms around him and cried. At first they were gentle tears, but soon the wave of emotions overtook her as her whole body shook. Warren cradled her in his arms and led her to the sofa. He placed her beside himself and held her tightly. Words wouldn't do. Tender compassion and God's grace were the only things that could minister to Kayla.

და

Kayla vaguely recalled Warren leading her to the couch. She sniffed and rubbed her eyes. The tears had stopped and she was once again in control. She nuzzled into his chest and murmured, "Thanks."

"Anytime."

"I'm sorry, I. . .I don't. . ."

"Shh, things like this just get to a person every so often. You've been a rock for Freda."

His gentle words equaled his touch as he pushed back her hair from her face. *A woman could get lost in this man's touch,* she thought. Then she bolted upright.

"Sorry." She fumbled, trying to straighten his damp shirt.

Warren chuckled. "No problem."

Kayla wiped her eyes and cheeks. "I must be a wreck."

Warren's voice cracked. "You look beautiful."

Kayla got up from the couch. "Can I get you a cold drink, iced tea perhaps?"

"Sure, I'd love some."

She shot to the kitchen as if her feet were on fire. How had she allowed herself to get lost in his arms? *After all, it's just Warren.*

Just Warren. She mulled that around for a bit. *And who is "just Warren"?* she thought. Her answer surprised her. The most caring man she'd ever met. How many times over the past ten months had he offered a hand, come to Freda's rescue, come to hers?

Maybe there was more to Warren Robinson than she'd previously understood.

Kayla glanced into the living room. His thin, lean body was hunched over with his elbows on his knees and hands clasped. His brown eyes were closed as if in prayer. Was he praying?

Probably for Freda. He truly loved her grandmother.

It had to be hard on him to see Freda in this state. But could Kayla put her in a home? Kayla touched her swollen eye. Maybe she didn't have a choice any longer.

The doorbell rang. "Who could it be at this hour?" She sprang toward the door with Warren's iced tea in her hand.

Warren jumped up from the couch.

"Brian?"

"Kayla. What happened to you?" Brian took one look at Kayla's eye, then looked over at Warren and groaned. "You no-good. . ."

Brian's fist missed Warren's face only because of the quick block Warren made.

"Brian, stop it. Warren didn't do it."

Brian eyeballed Warren and looked back at Kayla.

"Gram hit me with the phone. Accidentally," she added.

"You've got to put that woman in a home, Kayla." Brian released his fist and moved back toward Kayla.

"I'll put her in a home when the time is right." Kayla stamped her foot for emphasis—or frustration, she wasn't sure which.

"Look, I only came by to let you know Mack is on the up-and-up," Brian pleaded.

"I talked with my dad, Brian. He said to let Mr. Jefferies know the property isn't for sale and won't be for sale."

"I see." Brian looked back at Warren. "Don't you guys know this is progress?"

"People need food, Brian." Warren spoke up. "What's the country going to do when they eliminate all the farms? How are they going to feed themselves?"

"Ah, there'll always be farms. Just go farther west."

"You can only 'go west' for so long, Brian. There has to be a point in time when people realize they need farms rather than fancy houses on waterfront property."

"You just don't get it, Robinson. You can have your farm, and we can have those fancy waterfront houses. Both can live together."

"Not if your fancy houses start using up the water for the crops. Those houses require lots of water. Has Mack put a reservoir or a sewage treatment plant in his plans?"

Brian shuffled his feet. "Can't say I know for sure. But look at those places on the other side of the lake. Folks love it there."

"Yeah, and look how much more noise is on the lake. How many more people are using the lake for recreation? It's the drinking water for the farm animals and irrigation for the plants."

Kayla watched Warren become more determined.

"You can't decide everything on the dollar value. You have to decide on the overall greater good for the community."

"Bingo. Jefferies's project will bring in more jobs, a newer school, more revenue in taxes. The community will be much better off."

"I don't see it that way, Brian." Warren fetched his Stetson, tapped it on his right thigh, then placed it on his head. "Good night, Brian, Kayla. It's getting late. I'll see you tomorrow night when I come take care of Freda for your date."

Kayla stopped him before he made it to the kitchen door. She gently grabbed his left arm. "Thanks."

Warren winked and whispered, "You're welcome," and slipped outside.

Brian stood there wagging his head. "So, why won't your father sell?"

"Brian, Dad says it's premature to discuss this now with Gram still alive."

"How long do you think she'll hang on?"

He was as sensitive as a cold fish. Kayla placed her hands upon her hips. "You don't get it, do you?"

"What?"

"She's a human being, Brian. A live, breathing human being. She's always been here for her family. We can't just ignore her because she has some horrible brain disease."

"I didn't mean it that way. I was just asking so I could give Mack a time frame, is all."

Kayla sighed. "We don't know. Her body is in excellent health. The doctor says she could live for ten more years."

"Ten years? You'll saddle yourself with her for ten years?"

"Brian!" Kayla held back a yell.

He held his hands up in surrender. "Sorry. It's. . .well, it's just that I thought you and I might have something going and—well, I just can't imagine waiting ten years for you to be free of her."

Kayla closed her eyes and counted to three. "Brian, I'm not all that attracted to you. I mean, I enjoyed our date, but there wasn't any chemistry between us, you know?"

"I thought we had a great time." Brian knitted his blond eyebrows and slumped his well-defined shoulders. He had the body, that was for sure. So what was it that bothered her? His personality, lack of compassion? Compassion. That was it. He paled in comparison to Warren. Warren obviously knew the Lord. She wasn't sure about Brian.

His bright blue eyes pleaded for assurance. "Yes, I had fun. But, no, I'm not interested in anything more than a casual friendship."

"It's because of her, isn't it?"

Was it because she couldn't see herself getting involved with anyone while she was caring for Freda? "I don't know,

Brian. I don't think so."

"You're an attractive woman, Kayla, but you're overburdened with Freda. No one should put this on you."

"No one did. I did it to myself. I love her, Brian. Don't you understand?"

"She isn't the woman you love anymore. She isn't even the woman I knew growing up here. You've got to see that, don't you?"

"Of course I know that. But that doesn't change the fact that she's still my great-grandmother, and I love her."

"Look, I came over to tell you to dress really special tomorrow night. Mack is having a private party, and he invited me. But, honestly, I can't take you looking like this. By tomorrow that shiner will be black-and-blue. It just wouldn't do to have a woman on my arm with a black eye. Some might even think I did it."

"I understand. Consider the date canceled."

"Okay, if that's the way you want it." Brian headed for the front door.

If that's the way I want it? Kayla was liking Brian less and less as the minutes ticked by. "Good night, Brian."

"Night, Kayla. I'll call you."

"Sure." She waved him off and engaged the deadbolt behind him. She didn't want any more surprises. Today had had more than enough.

૨૯

The next evening Warren picked up Tim Daniels and drove his pickup to Kayla's. "Now remember, Tim, Freda gets nervous around strangers."

"Gotcha. Sure is a shame. She was always a spitfire at the local games."

Warren chuckled. "Yeah, she was that."

"So what's in it for you, helping out Freda Brown?"

"Nothing, just being neighborly."

"You ain't getting paid?" Tim turned in the cab and faced Warren.

"Nope."

"Then who's paying me?"

"I am." Warren snatched a glimpse of Tim from the corner of his eye.

Tim's blond eyebrows knit together in the center of his forehead. "Why?"

"Because I could use some help, and you need to get started saving for that computer."

"But your own pocket?" Tim wagged his head from side to side. "My old man would never fork over his hard-earned cash if he weren't being paid."

Warren let the comment about Tim's father drop. "It's like this—a computer is a good thing to have. But a man needs to understand the worth of something in order to really appreciate it. If your dad just gave you a computer, you'd enjoy it, maybe even do some good with it, but you wouldn't take care of it the same way you will once you see how hard it is to work for something like a computer."

"Maybe. Never bought anything before with my own money." Tim slid back into the bench seat of the pickup's cab and looked straight ahead.

"Well then, it's time you start. Part of growing up is being responsible, working a job, earning pay for it. That's the first step toward being responsible."

"I do my chores on the farm. I know how to work."

"Didn't say you don't. However, when I pay you at the end of the night, you can tell me how it feels."

"That's a no-brainer. It will be awesome."

Warren chuckled. "Yeah, it's pretty awesome."

Warren pulled up to the front of the small farmhouse. Kayla waved from the front porch.

Tim whistled. "Man. Who clobbered her?"

nine

Kayla ached in places she didn't even know she had muscles. Warren and Tim worked hard while Kayla tried to keep up. It amazed her how two men could move such heavy furniture so easily, not to mention pull up flooring. Thankfully, Freda's hearing loss kept her oblivious of the activity going on in her kitchen. Kayla kept the door closed while Freda watched her merry-go-round show.

Pulling up the linoleum proved to be more of a task than first expected. Sometime in the past, long before Kayla had any memory of it, the flooring had been laid over another layer of cracked linoleum. That meant pulling out nails as well as ripping up the still-glued sections.

Kayla rubbed her sore back. Freda now slept quietly in the back bedroom. "You guys up for a break?"

"Yeah," Tim called out. "This is hard work."

Warren grinned. "Sure, got any cold drinks?"

"Iced tea or fresh lemonade. Take your pick," Kayla offered.

Drinks poured, the three of them sat at the dining room table. Kayla rubbed the chilled glass across her forehead before taking a sip. The cool nectar rolled down her tongue as she gulped. Tim downed his glass and poured another from the pitcher without saying a word. Warren sipped his slowly after closing his eyes for a brief—what? prayer? Immediately, Kayla silently offered a prayer of thanks for lemons, ice, and sugar.

The phone jangled her back to the room and the people around her. She leaned around and grabbed the phone. "Hello?"

"Kayla, I've just received a very disturbing message." Her

father's words were tight. His tone was too familiar: He was angry but trying to control his temper.

"What's the matter, Daddy?" Kayla glanced at Tim and Warren.

"What's the matter? I hear from a perfect stranger that my daughter is sporting a black eye the size of half her face, and you've the gall to ask me what's the matter?"

"Daddy, calm down. I'm fine. It was an accident." Kayla turned her back to the men.

"Kayla, I told you if Gram gets violent she's going to a home."

"No. It wasn't like that. Who told you?" She'd been praying all day, trying to decide if it was time for Freda to be hospitalized or not. She'd even called the doctor. Paranoia was very common in patients with Alzheimer's, and he had offered some medications that would help control it, if needed.

Kayla heard her father rustling through the pages on his desk. "A Mr. Brian Jackson."

Kayla groaned. "Dad, I don't know what Brian told you, but we had a date tonight and he was really upset with me. He broke the date because he didn't want to be seen with a woman who had a black eye. He's concerned about himself, not me, not Gram. In fact, he's working with the land developers who want to buy the land from Gram."

"Interesting."

"Dad, Gram simply got confused. She was scared and tried to call the police. I shouldn't have tried to take the phone from her. Thankfully, Warren arrived, and he helped calm her."

"Robinson?"

"Yes."

"Interesting."

"You keep saying that. Why?"

"Mr. Jackson said he had an offer he'd like to discuss with me, but we didn't talk about it over the phone. I figured it was about the land, and I didn't intend to call him back. But the note about you and your black eye bothered me. He claimed Freda did it."

"Wellll, she did, but she didn't. It was the phone that actually hit me, and she wasn't trying to hit me with it. She just thought I was someone else, and she wanted to call the police."

"Has this happened before?"

"No, Gram's never gotten frightened when she's not recognized me. Most of the time she thinks I'm someone she knows or one of several Kaylas in her life. I think I'm up to three people now."

Her father chuckled. Kayla released her pent-up breath. "Trust me, Daddy. If Gram needs to go to a home, I'll put her in one."

"I'm just afraid you'll be too close to her, Princess, that you'll lose perspective."

"Would it help if you talked with Warren?"

"Is he there?"

"Yes, he and Tim Daniels are pulling up the kitchen floor."

"That's tonight, I forgot. Sure, put Warren on. I'd like to thank him."

"Okay." Kayla turned around. "Warren, my father would like to speak to you."

"No problem." Warren put down his glass and stepped beside her. He placed his hand on her shoulder and whispered, "Everything will be fine."

Kayla nodded and handed the phone to him. His hand still rested on her shoulder, protective, reassuring. She didn't want to pull away, but it seemed intrusive to stand right beside him while he spoke with her father.

"Hello. . . Yes, Sir. . . No, Sir. . . Yes. . . No." Warren laughed. "It's a beaut."

Kayla cringed and sat at the table.

Tim spoke up. "Someone told your father about Freda bopping you?"

Kayla rolled her eyes. "She didn't, the phone did."

"Whatever. Seems odd to hear adults tattling."

"Tell me about it. Apparently, someone wants Gram's land more than I thought."

"Ah, been a lot of folks being asked to sell. Price is good. Pa hasn't decided to sell yet, though. He's not sure he can do anything but farm, and why sell a farm just to buy another one someplace else?"

"Your father is a wise man."

"Sometimes." Tim looked over at Warren who was hanging up the phone. "He's not holding off like Warren and his folks, because they want to do what's right. He's just holding off because he isn't sure it's good for him."

"I see."

And Kayla was seeing. In a few short days, Warren was leaving his mark on this young man. And by the lopsided grin on Warren's face, Kayla figured he had reassured her father as well. Brian Jackson, while he had the great exterior and good looks, had an interior that was sorely lacking. And Warren, while he wasn't well endowed in the looks department, had a heart that spoke volumes of the man's character, ethics, and love. She thought of the biblical passage that spoke of Jesus not being the most handsome of men. . . Kayla glanced back at Warren. *He* is *handsome, in his own way,* she mused. She had a strange desire to run her fingers through his rich mahogany brown hair.

❧

Warren glanced at Kayla. If he didn't know better, he'd swear she was sizing him up. Her green eyes sparkled with excitement. She was staring. Her cheeks flamed. Then she distracted herself with her drink. *Odd,* Warren pondered. She'd just looked at him the way she'd looked at and relished her first sip of lemonade earlier this evening. *Attraction? From Kayla?*

"You're off the hook, Kayla."

She whipped her head back and glanced at him.

"Your father believes you."

"I wish he'd come and visit. Then these foolish calls wouldn't be necessary."

"Perhaps." Warren placed his hand on Tim's shoulder. "Are you up for a couple more hours?"

"You bet." Tim jumped from the table, springing into life.

To be a teen again with unlimited strength and endurance. Warren wagged his head. Nope, going through the teen years once was enough. "Let's go."

Warren placed his hand on top of Kayla's. Her eyes caught his. "We need to talk."

She nodded but didn't say a word. He gently squeezed her hand before releasing it. "Speak to the Lord, Kayla," he whispered. Then he turned back to Tim. "Let's haul the old linoleum into my truck first, Tim. It'll give us a better idea of what's left."

"Sure."

They worked for two more hours. Finally, the old flooring was off. Kayla had joined them shortly after giving herself a few minutes to compose herself and her thoughts. She worked hard, and she was covered from head to foot with dust and dirt. Warren's fingers itched to remove the smudge on her right cheek. . . Not that his hands were any cleaner. He'd probably just make it worse.

"Ready to go home, Tim?"

"Yeah, but I can work some more, if you need it."

"Thanks, but I've had it for the night. Got to feed the animals early in the morning."

Tim groaned. Apparently, a similar fate awaited him in the morning. Warren slapped him on the back. "It's not that bad."

"Yeah, easy for you to say. You went to college and had a four-year break."

Kayla straightened. "College?"

Warren grinned. "Yeah. I'm an agricultural engineer."

"I didn't know."

Tim interrupted. "He got all the fancy new information about farming. Do you know he's doing something different with rotating the crops on his southern field?"

"No, I didn't know that. Apparently, there's more to Mr. Robinson than meets the eye." Kayla winked.

"You can say that. Did you know he was paying me?" Tim squared his shoulders.

"Yeah, I knew that."

"Do you know why?" Tim asked.

"Saving for a computer, I believe." Kayla smiled. "What kind do you want to get?"

"Been real interested in the new Macs. The cube looks cool, but I think I'll need more ports, so I'm looking at the G4s."

"Are you interested in web programming and design?" Kayla asked. Warren wondered if that was Kayla's college degree. She seemed right up on "the cube," whatever that was.

"Hope to. Just not sure if I have the brains for it. I mean, the technology keeps growing so fast."

"True, but if you apply yourself, and if it's the kind of thing that comes natural to you, you'll do fine."

Warren interrupted. "Personally, I'm a PC kind of guy— who needs sleep. So if you two can stop talking computers long enough to say good night, we'll be off."

"Sorry," Kayla offered sheepishly. "Thanks, Tim, for all your help tonight."

"No problem. Sorry we couldn't get the job done."

Kayla turned to Warren and placed her hand on his back. "Thanks, Warren."

Her gentle touch sent a warm wave across his muscles, releasing some of the strain and tension. "I'll be by tomorrow after everything is settled at the farm."

Kayla nodded her head and gently pushed him out the door. "Good night."

"Are we heading to the dump first?" Tim asked, pulling himself up into the cab of the truck.

"If you're up for it." Warren fished his keys from his pocket. The cool night air was a welcome relief from the heat and exercise. Who was he kidding? Ever since Kayla looked at him like he was a chocolate ice cream cone, his mind and emotions had worked overtime; his face still burned.

Tim broke the silence as they drove down the dirt driveway. "Kayla's pretty."

"Yeah."

"She's smart, too. Not many folks know about the cube."

Warren figured he fell into the not-many-folks crowd and nodded, keeping a watchful eye on the dark road. Two beams of light penetrated the near-black area.

Tim chuckled. "You don't either, do you?"

" 'Fraid not. What is it?"

Tim went on to explain the new computer that uses technology and runs so cool it doesn't need a fan. *Has to be platinum rather than gold on the circuit boards,* Warren assessed. "Eight by eight, huh?"

"Yep, eight inches by eight inches. It's totally awesome."

"I bet."

They continued talking computers, the pluses and minuses of the various kinds. Tim honestly had a deep love for the machine, Warren realized, working with them at school and at the library, but the boy would flourish with one at home.

After a brief stop at the town dump, Warren brought Tim home. In the driveway, he pulled out his wallet. "Here, Tim. You were a big help tonight." Counting out three twenties, he handed the folded bills to Tim.

Warren grinned as the boy put them into his pocket without counting them. He knew Tim would have them whipped out of his shirt pocket the second Warren pulled out of his driveway.

Warren extended his hand and gave him a firm handshake. "Thanks, Tim."

"You're welcome. Do you need some help tomorrow?"

Warren held back a snicker. "Thanks for the offer, but I'll be fine."

"Okay, thanks again." Tim slipped out of the cab and shut the door. "Night." He tapped the door and bounced toward the front steps of his house.

Warren popped the truck into gear and headed home. He was stiff and sore all over. He prayed his father would give him a hand tomorrow. Tonight had proved to be a much bigger job than he'd anticipated.

He pulled into the driveway, cutting the engine and rolling in close to the house, not wanting to wake his folks. It was midnight, and they would have gone to bed hours ago. In his room, he stripped down to his waist and headed for the shower. One look in the mirror, and he marveled at all the dirt. His hair even stood up straight in some places.

The shower proved to be a welcome relief to his protesting muscles. He'd always thought of himself as being in good shape. Tonight he suspected that simply wasn't the case.

Clean and bone weary, he plopped on his bed and fired up a quick prayer for his day. His eyes closed. His mind drifted. Memories of hungry green eyes sparkling in his direction gave him hope and fear. Could he possibly measure up? He needed to go slow. He needed to be patient. He needed sleep. Exhausted, Warren groaned into his pillow, knowing he still wouldn't be able to sleep.

At last, his breathing slowed. . .just as an explosion rocked the night air. Warren jumped out of bed and ran to a window.

ten

Kayla jumped out of bed. "What was that?" She glanced through her back window and saw a ball of fire rising in the night sky, coming from across the lake near the new housing development. "Oh, Lord, keep everyone safe."

She scurried to the phone and placed a call to 911. Naturally, she wasn't the only one who had called in the alarm.

Pacing for twenty minutes didn't change the reality of the explosion, nor could she help. The most she could do was pray. After a few minutes of prayer, exhaustion from the long night of working on the floor took hold, and she drifted off to sleep.

❧

The next morning she learned that a transformer for the new development had blown. No foul play was suspected, and an investigation was under way.

Warren came by around noon with his dad, and the two men finished off the floor while Kayla took Freda to town.

"Gram, would you like to stop for coffee?"

"Coffee would be nice." Freda clenched her handbag in her lap.

Kayla drove to a diner and helped her great-grandmother out of the car.

"Hello, Freda." An older gentleman with a bald pate and rounding waistline smiled.

"Hello?" Freda's eyes darted from the stranger to Kayla. This was the hard part about taking Freda out. She'd meet people she should know but didn't remember. Her eyes darkened with fear.

"Hi, Sam. Quite an explosion last night, huh?"

"I'll say. Woke up the whole town. Several folks over on Richmond's land are out of power."

"I can imagine." Kayla supported Freda. Her ability to balance herself had waned in recent days. Kayla made a mental note to mention it to Gram's doctors.

"Good to see you, Freda. Always a pleasure." Sam reached out his hand.

Freda grasped it. "Good to see you, too, Robert."

Sam's eyes lit up. "Miss you, Freda. God bless you."

Kayla's eyes watered. A small town knew everyone's business, and the realization that everyone knew Freda had Alzheimer's was strangely comforting.

"God bless you, too, Kayla. You're doing a fine job. Don't you go listening to anyone's gossip."

"Gossip?"

"Your shiner has the town buzzing. Word is—" He cleared his throat and lowered his voice. "That Freda did it."

"Ah, actually it was the phone." Kayla grinned. "But, yes, she did have a confused moment. Warren Robinson came over and helped calm her."

"Such a shame. She was such a spitfire."

Kayla laughed out loud. "Still is, sometimes."

Sam stifled a laugh and his belly shook with joy. "I can see that. Bye." He waved as he departed, slipping into his old pickup truck.

Inside the diner, with its fifties-style old Formica tabletops edged in chrome, Freda sipped her coffee and played with the edges of her napkin.

"What's the matter, Gram?"

"I've forgotten that man's name," she mumbled.

"It's okay, Gram."

"I'd just as soon have the good Lord take me now."

Kayla placed her hand on top of her grandmother's. Her own frustrations with death and dying and this horrible disease resurfaced. *It doesn't seem fair somehow to have a person suffer so. But to be honest, what disease is fair?* "I know, Gram. The good Lord will take you when the time is right."

"I am not afraid of dying. But I've seen enough to remember old folks going senile. Am I senile, Kayla?"

"Alzheimer's, Gram, another form of dementia."

"That's the bad one, right?"

"Yes."

"Figures." Freda sipped her coffee. "Who gave you that shiner?"

"I ran into the phone."

Freda shook her head. "You young folks are always rushing."

Kayla chuckled. "Yeah, I guess we do."

Moments of confusion, moments of clarity, balled into moments like today. *Are these precious few moments of clarity for me or Gram?* Kayla wondered. She reached for her diet drink, then left it there. Her stomach couldn't handle it at the moment. The bitter reality of what was in store for Freda sharpened in her mind's eye. *Oh, God, please, don't let her suffer.*

&

"Looks good, Son." George patted Warren on the back.

"Thanks for your help, Dad." Freda's new floor glistened.

"Not a problem. Anything to help out a neighbor." George stood back and folded his arms across his chest. "How bad is Freda?"

"She has her moments." Warren finished sweeping up the debris.

"That shiner is something."

Warren nodded. "She clocked Kayla good. I'm surprised she didn't get knocked out."

"Looks painful. But, Son, does Freda need to go into a home?"

"I don't think she does just yet. But Kayla knows if Freda keeps up this kind of behavior, she'll have no choice. The doc did prescribe some meds to help."

"Good. I don't want to see anyone getting hurt, especially Freda."

"Yeah, I hear you." Warren tapped the dustpan inside the trash can. "Well, I think we can go home now."

"Great, let's swing by the housing development and look at the damage."

"All right." The men closed the door and headed to the truck.

The development looked fine, and, remarkably, there was little scorching from the fire on the transformer. The concrete base the transformer sat on extended several feet out beyond the actual fenced-in area. "Looks like it blew itself out," George observed.

"Appears so. Fortunately it didn't spark to anyone's home."

An enterprising young man, perhaps all of eight years, sat at a lemonade stand. When Warren's gaze reached the blond boy with smudges on his face, the boy called out, "Want some ice-cold lemonade?"

"Sure. How much?"

"A dollar."

"A dollar? Pretty expensive."

"Yeah, well, my mom only had these really big glasses left, and they fit four of the little ones."

"I see. I'll take two." Warren pulled his wallet out of his pocket.

"Thanks, Mister." His grin was exaggerated by large teeth. But he was young and would be growing into those teeth one day.

Warren handed over the two dollars and picked up his two

glasses of lemonade. "How are your sales?"

"Great. Folks coming from all over to see this."

"Did you see it last night?" Warren asked.

"Sure did. The whole house shook. A ball of fire as big as a baseball field shot up into the sky. It was awesome."

"I bet. Do your folks have power yet?"

"Don't know. I suppose so by now. The electric company had men over all morning."

"Have a good day." Warren passed his father a glass.

George pointed to a charred bird lying between two of the transformers. "Bet that's what caused the problem."

"Bet you're right."

George removed his ball cap and wiped his brow. "Still seems odd a tiny critter like that could cause such an explosion."

Warren looked back at the bird and above it. Yeah, it was odd, since these things were built to keep out people and animals who weren't supposed to be there. They drove home in silence. Warren wondered what, if anything, the bird had to do with the explosion.

Later that evening, Warren talked briefly with Kayla on the phone. She seemed very pleased and appreciative of the work he'd done. She even expressed a desire to do something special for him. Warren's problem was, all he wanted was a tender embrace and a kiss. But that he'd never ask for.

❧

Kayla spoke with the pastor briefly after the Sunday morning service. Due to the progression of Freda's Alzheimer's, Kayla didn't feel she could continue teaching the children at Sunday school. She foresaw many days in the future when Freda wouldn't be able to go to church at all.

The kids were excited about planting their mustard seeds. Most having been raised on a farm, they understood the principle of a small seed becoming a large plant. She finally decided to share that the kingdom of heaven was growing inside each of them, and as they planted a seed in other people's hearts about Jesus and His kingdom, the seed grew. She still felt it was a hard concept for little ones to understand. But the picture of a large plant growing from a little seed; that was easy.

As for herself, she saw how her great-grandmother's strong faith had affected her entire family for four generations. Could Kayla's faith have the same profound effect on her own children, grandchildren, and great-grandchildren? She didn't know, but she prayed it would. Of course, she'd need to get a husband first. Kayla grinned.

"Did you have a good time at church, Gram?"

"Fine. Preacher talked too long."

Kayla chuckled. "Are you hungry?"

Freda nodded.

"Would you like to go out to eat or eat at home?"

"Home." Freda sat facing the front of the car, *a sentry without a post,* Kayla reflected.

"Home it is, Gram." Personally, Kayla would have loved to go out to dinner, but she understood this once very social lady no longer appreciated crowds. Perhaps the confusion was intensified when she was among strangers.

Freda's bony fingers clutched her purse. Something was wrong. Kayla knew it with every fiber of her being, but what? How do you fight shadows and images in another person's mind?

"Gram?"

Freda didn't respond.

"Gram?" she called a little louder.

Freda turned her head, her eyes wide with fear. Kayla pulled over to the side of the road. "Oh, Gram, it's okay. Trust me, everything is okay."

"Those men were after me."

"What men?"

"Back there—they had dark coats. They wanted my money. I didn't give it to them."

"It's okay now, Gram. They're gone now."

Freda's nose flared; the pulse on her neck beat wildly. "No, they're going to come after me. Bring me home."

Should she take her home or to the hospital? Kayla positioned herself back behind the steering wheel and patted Freda's hand. "I'll protect you, Gram. No one will come after you now."

Freda grasped her hand. The fear was real, even if the reason for the fears was not. The only thing Kayla could figure was the collection of the offering scared her. Yes, telling the pastor she could no longer teach the children had been the right thing to do.

At the house, Kayla made a quick lunch of toasted cheese sandwiches and tomato soup. Freda ate most of her meal, then lay down for a nap.

As soon as she was down, Kayla tapped out Warren's phone number, praying he was home. She needed to talk. And she needed to talk with someone who understood. Warren was the only one. When he had become her anchor she didn't know, but she knew now she needed him. The phone rang and rang. On the fourth ring, the answering machine came on. Should she leave a message?

Kayla started to put the phone back in the cradle, then pulled it back to her ear. She waited for the appropriate tone, and spoke. "Warren, this is Kayla. If you've got a minute, please call me. Freda's getting worse. I need to talk."

She placed the phone back in the receiver and paced. Did she need to send Gram into a home? *Has she gotten that much worse, so quickly?* "Father, help me. I don't know what to do."

The doorbell rang, interrupting her thoughts.

Kayla went to the door. "Brian?"

"Hi; can I come in?"

"No, I don't think so." Kayla didn't want to deal with Brian Jackson at the moment. Not now, possibly not ever.

Brian's broad shoulders slumped. "Kayla, I'm sorry about the other night. I was out of line. I feel bad; please let me apologize."

"Apology accepted."

He raised his head and looked straight into her eyes. "I thought—" He moved a step closer. "I thought we might be able to start again."

"Brian, I'm really not attracted to you. You're a nice enough guy and all, but there's no chemistry."

"Kayla, just give me a little time. I'll grow on you."

Like a bad rash, she quipped to herself. "Brian, Freda's getting worse. I don't have time for dating."

Brian took in a deep breath; his neck grew a shade darker, but he held his tongue. "All right. Will you at least consider me after you've put her in a home?"

Not even if he were the last man on earth, she warned herself. "I have no prospects at the moment, and I'm not looking to get involved with anyone."

"Good." Brian clasped her shoulders and pulled her into his embrace and kissed her head. "I thought I ruined my chances."

You have, she wanted to scream. She pushed her hands against his chest and got herself free. "I'm really not interested."

"That's okay, little lady. I'll grow on you, wait and see."

Kayla fought the urge to roll back her eyes. *Oh, Lord, put a woman in this man's path who is right for him, and get him out of mine,* she silently prayed.

"Kayla?" Warren called from inside the house.

Relief warmed her.

Fire ignited in Brian's eyes. "Not interested, huh?"

eleven

"Good-bye, Brian." Warren heard Kayla's voice whistle around her teeth. A desire to protect her made Warren stand behind her as a reinforcement.

Brian's gaze locked with Warren's. "Are you always here?"

"Nope, only when she needs me." Warren grinned. He'd heard voices when he had entered the kitchen, and he hadn't liked the tone he had heard from Brian.

Brian huffed and stormed down the front walkway toward his car. Warren turned to Kayla. "What was that all about?"

"Nothing."

"Kayla, that wasn't nothing. The two of you looked like lions about to pounce."

"He just won't take no for an answer."

No? She's ended her relationship with Brian?

Tears pooled in her eyes, and his heart leapt to his throat. "Oh, Kayla," he whispered and pulled her into his chest. She buried her face in his chest. "Shh, it's going to be okay," he promised.

For the second time in less than a week, he felt Kayla allow herself to open up to him. *Lord, give her strength*, Warren silently prayed.

"I'm sorry. I don't usually fall apart like this." She sniffled and pulled herself from his embrace.

He wanted to pull her back. "You've been under a lot of stress."

"I suppose."

"Kayla, let's sit and talk about what happened today."

"I don't want to talk about Brian."

"Neither do I. I'm referring to the phone message I received, something about Freda." He leaned down and pushed a stray strand of auburn hair from her face.

Kayla looked up at him and searched his eyes, her gaze penetrating deep into his soul. "And we need to talk about us. . .what's happening between us," he said.

She shifted her gaze to the floor.

"Tell me what happened with Freda." Holding her hand, Warren led her to the couch. She followed and sat down.

Pulling a throw pillow to her chest, she hugged it. "She was afraid again. She thought some men were trying to steal her money in church. I think it was during the offering, but I'm not sure."

Warren chuckled.

"It's not funny." Kayla's lip twitched, though, as if against her will.

"Sure, it is. Look at it this way. Freda was probably one of the most generous people I ever knew. And here she is at church, hanging on to her wallet."

"I suppose. But still, it's paranoia, isn't it?"

"I guess. Did she get violent?"

"No, but she was scared, Warren. I saw the terror in her eyes. She really believed those men were out to get her—or rather, her money."

"How much did she have?"

She knitted her eyebrows, and he fought the desire to run his fingers through her hair. "Ten dollars, at the most. I'm not sure."

"Hmm, the great church thieves. They hit up the old ladies for ten bucks."

Kayla whacked him with a pillow. "Stop it. I'm serious."

Warren sobered. "I know, and I don't like the fact that she's more delusional. Did you give her the new meds?"

"Yes, but they seem to make her more lethargic."

They fell silent, while the quiet moments passed. Warren hoped that Kayla could feel God's peace comforting her heart.

❧

When at last Warren moved, he leaned back, one arm straddled the back of the couch, his hand mere inches from her arm. Kayla fought the desire to lean up against him. He was right, they needed to talk about this attraction. But first she needed to decide what to do about Gram.

"Have you looked into some of the nursing homes in the area?"

"A little, not much. Do you think it's time?"

"I think she's getting there, yes. I've heard that once these paranoia situations begin, patients with Alzheimer's become less and less of themselves, markedly so, each day."

"She sure has started to regress quickly this week. The funny thing is, when I took her out to the diner yesterday, she had another one of those clarity moments. It's so baffling."

"How's the bladder control?"

"Just about shot, and she's starting to have trouble controlling her bowels."

Warren nodded and placed his hand on hers. "I don't know how much longer you'll be able to take care of her, Kayla."

"I was thinking about hiring a nurse to come during the day so I can get a break. That way she'll still be in her own home."

"Can you afford it?"

"No. My dad can. But she's entitled to more aid if we put her in an institution than if we keep her in her own home. It doesn't seem right."

"No, it's not right. But we're dealing with a worldly system, not a Christ-centered one."

Kayla pondered Warren's response. In many ways, he was

right. The world's system worked by impersonalizing everyone. God cared so uniquely about everyone He bothered to count the hairs on their heads and knew a person down to his or her DNA structure. "You know, I never thought of it quite like that before."

"So, what can I do to help?" Warren traced his finger over her left hand.

Kayla closed her eyes and tried to focus. *Why does he affect me so?*

"Kayla," he whispered.

"Hmm?"

"I want to kiss you. May I?" His voice shivered down her spine. She leaned into him; he pulled her toward him. She wasn't sure who did what, she just knew she was now leaning into his embrace, anticipating a kiss.

A kiss? Kayla flung her eyes open and pulled away.

Warren opened his sinfully chocolate eyes. Why did she love chocolate, dark chocolate, so much? She groaned.

The corners of his lips turned up slightly. He'd seen her response. "I'll wait, Darling."

"Warren, I like you."

"Shh, don't go spoiling the moment by talking. I saw the desire in your eyes, and I know you saw it in mine. I'm a patient man, Kayla. I can wait."

"This is crazy. I've seen you almost every day for ten months. Why now? Why all of a sudden?"

"Don't know. I've been waiting a long time." Warren's cheeks flushed from his admission.

"Long time?" Kayla barely got the words out.

"Yes. Kayla, I've prayed long and hard. I've been attracted to you, and you've not shown the slightest interest in me. I must say, to see it in your eyes now sure does boost a man's ego."

Kayla couldn't believe her ears or her eyes. For months, he

was simply the farmer from next door. Pleasant enough, helpful even, but now. . . What stirred within her? Desire? Some maybe, but was it deeper than that? It wasn't just a need to be close to him. There was something in who he was as a person that drew her to him. Why hadn't she seen these qualities in him before? Why was she seeing them now? It just didn't make sense.

"Pray, Kayla. Ask the Lord what's happening to you, to me. Is there a future for us? Ask. He'll guide you."

"But I went to school to work in the city for a large corporation doing computer consulting, system analysis. This area doesn't need that. You're a farmer. You like it. You want to stay here."

"I know, didn't make sense to me either." He cupped her hand in his. "But God doesn't put the wrong people together. If He's leading us to get together, He'll work out the details."

"Would you consider not farming?"

"Don't think so, but I will pray about it. That is, if you decide you want to get involved with someone like me."

"Goodness, Warren. You're honest, dependable, and no one could want a better neighbor."

"Ah, but I want more than that, Kayla. I want love, passion, all those things that make up a good and healthy marriage. I want a friendship first. What you just described could be attributed to the family dog. I won't settle for a relationship where we aren't 100 percent sold out on the idea of wanting to be together because we love each other that much."

"I. . .I. . ." What could she say? He was as dependable as a golden retriever. Granted, there was some chemistry developing between them, but marriage? No way—not now. Possibly not later. *This is Warren!*

"I'm not a man who's built like Brian Jackson, but I am a

man. And men need and want certain things from a relationship, Kayla. Security, love, commitment. I can't settle for anything less. Will you pray?"

Kayla nodded. Of course she'd pray. She was about to do that right now.

Warren's strong callused hands clasped Kayla's. He prayed, "Father, we open our hearts and minds to Your will for us. We lift Freda before You and the decisions Kayla needs to make. Guide her, Lord. Show her what is right, and when and if she should put Freda into a home. Give her peace. And, Lord, direct us both about these feelings and desires we have for each other. Nurture them with Your Holy Spirit so they become sanctified by You. Lead us in the path You would have us go, not in some path the world or even our own sinful natures would choose. Guide us, Lord. In Jesus' name, amen."

"Amen." Kayla released a pent-up breath. "Warren, I need more time."

"I know, Darling. I'll wait." He pulled her hands to his mouth and tenderly kissed her fingers. "God is good, Kayla. He'll lead you, and He'll lead me."

"I needed to talk with you tonight about Gram. I didn't want to talk with anyone but you. You've become very special to me, Warren. I hope you understand that."

"I do." Warren mustered every ounce of strength he could and rose from the couch. "I need to go, Kayla. Unless you need me to stay?"

"No, I'm fine now. I think." She winked.

"Yeah, I feel the same way." He grabbed his Stetson from the table and plopped it on his head. "Night, Ma'am," he drawled in the best John Wayne accent he could.

Kayla laughed. Its lively lilt was music to his ears. He'd openly confessed his feelings for her tonight. He couldn't believe he'd shared so much. The question was, had he said too much too soon?

"Warren," Kayla called as his hand reached the doorknob.

He popped his head around the doorway to the kitchen. "Kayla?"

Slowly, she crossed the room and came up beside him. "Thanks for coming over tonight."

"Anytime, just call."

"Warren, I—"

A thud came from Freda's room. Kayla turned and ran. He fought trampling her to get to Freda. Sprawled on the floor near the bed, Freda moaned.

"Gram." Kayla's voice trembled.

Warren knelt down beside Freda. "Where's it hurt?"

"My legs, my hips."

"Oh, no, Lord." Kayla ran back to the other room and dialed what he assumed was 911.

Warren lightly touched Freda's legs. There was no evidence of broken bones, but elderly bones often snapped.

"Hang on, Freda. Help's on the way."

Tears streamed down Freda's face. Warren placed a pillow under her head. He fussed with her nightgown, giving her a modest appearance.

"Ambulance is on its way. How is she?"

"In pain."

Kayla knelt beside her grandmother. "Oh, Gram, what happened?"

Warren stepped back and gave her room. Kayla brushed the gray hair from Freda's face.

"I fell." Freda's voice strained from the pain. "Oh, God, take away the pain."

twelve

Kayla paced up and down the antiseptic hall of the hospital. She had ridden in the ambulance with Freda. Warren arrived shortly after in his truck. The X-rays showed a fractured right femur, but her hips were fine. Normal treatment for a young healthy person would be bed rest and crutches. For a ninety-two-year-old woman—Kayla wasn't sure what the treatment would be. The doctors sedated Freda and put a brace on her leg. The lights, the ambulance, and the pain all caused Freda to become frightened again.

Warren made a round of calls. Gram would be staying a couple days in the hospital for observation. The hospital staff wanted to do a psychiatric evaluation. Not that it was necessary, in Kayla's mind. Freda had Alzheimer's. What else could they tell her?

Warren walked toward her. His Stetson and cowboy boots made quite an impressive sight. The man was tall—skinny, but tall—she had to give him that. She wrapped her arms around him as he enveloped her within his. "Come on, Darling, let's set you down and talk."

"She's fractured her femur."

"Which bone is that, the upper thigh or the thin one below the knee?"

"Upper thigh."

"Gotcha. Will she have a cast up to her hip?" Warren led her to a couple of chairs in the corner of the waiting room.

"No, a brace and a wheelchair. They don't like to put an elderly person's delicate skin in a cast. How'd she fall so hard?"

"I don't know, Kayla, but it's not your fault."

"But. . ." How could she tell him that she had suspected for a while that Gram needed a walker?

"Shh, you know better. This kind of thing could have happened at any time."

"But I noticed she was getting unsteady on her feet. I should have insisted she use a walker."

"Kayla." Warren tenderly pulled her chin upward. "Look at me. Honey, she wouldn't have remembered to use it."

He's so logical, Lord. "You're right. I just feel bad."

"Of course, you do. Anyone would. No one wants to see another person suffer."

"If I can't get a visiting nurse out to the farm daily, I'll have to put her in a home. She'll hate it, Warren, absolutely hate it."

"Yes, Freda would. But how much does the woman in the ER resemble Freda? She's a frightened old lady. Freda stood her ground. No one could bowl that woman over. This one, well, this isn't Freda."

"It hurts so much. I hate seeing her like this." Tears burned the edges of her eyelids. She wouldn't cry, not again.

Warren cradled her in his arms. "I'm here for you, Darling. The Lord's here, too, and He hurts just as much, if not more, for Freda."

Kayla breathed deeply. Warren's fresh scent filled her nostrils. She was becoming addicted to this man. His gentle wisdom, his loving care with people—what was holding her back from moving forward in a relationship with him?

Marriage. He had talked marriage, at least the possibility of it. He wasn't what she wanted in a husband. Was he? But wouldn't she want a husband in whom she found strength and comfort just being in his arms? Who calmed her soul simply by his touch? "We've got to stop doing this," Kayla whispered.

"Only if you insist. But I kinda like holding you." Warren

kissed the top of her head. It was ever so gentle, a bare whisper of a kiss. But she knew it because she felt it down to the tip of her toes. Is that why she'd stopped the kiss earlier this evening?

"Ms. Brown?" A man of medium height with a large nose and silver-rimmed glasses called from the doorway of the waiting room.

"Yes, Doctor?"

"Your grandmother is resting peacefully. We've braced the leg, but she won't be able to walk. I've ordered a wheelchair for her when she leaves. She's in the midstages of Alzheimer's, isn't she?"

"Yes, possibly beginning the later stages."

The doctor pushed up his glasses and sat down beside her. "She'll need to stay for a few days so we can see how she reacts to the brace. You might have to put her in a convalescent home." He scanned the chart. "I see you are her primary caregiver, and she lives with you."

"Yes."

"The chart says she fell in her bedroom. Is that correct?" The doctor looked over the rim of his glasses.

Kayla gave him a brief account of the accident and how she'd found her.

"Is she incontinent?" He held his pen over the chart.

"Yes, and recently started having trouble with her bowels. Bladder control she lost months ago, perhaps six."

The doctor nodded and wrote. "She's in great physical health otherwise, but I'm sure you knew that. Her heart is strong."

"She seemed more unsteady on her feet the past couple of days," Kayla offered.

"Then I must prepare you for the likelihood she may never leave the wheelchair. And, if that is the case, bedsores will develop if you don't keep moving her."

"I understand. Is there an agency you would recommend for in-home nursing care?"

The doctor flipped through the pages again. "I see you live in a pretty rural area."

Kayla nodded.

"I'll instruct the staff to give you some numbers of various agencies in your area. But it's late. You need to go home and rest. There isn't anything you can do for Freda now."

"May I see her before I go?" Kayla implored.

"Sure, five minutes. She's sleeping. Try not to wake her."

"Thanks."

"When you come back tomorrow, she'll be in her own room. Good night, Ms. Brown."

Kayla shook his hand and held Warren's hand as they approached Freda's bed in the ER. A white hospital gown, peppered with tiny blue flowers or something, was draped over Freda. An IV was taped to her left hand. The monitor beeped in the steady rhythm of her heart, and a gentle snore brought a smile to Kayla. "Thank You, Lord. She's going to be all right."

Warren embraced Kayla and whispered into her ear. "Give her a kiss and tell her you love her."

Kayla kissed Freda's forehead and whispered into her deaf ear. "I love you, Gram. I'll see you tomorrow. Good night."

❧

Warren held Freda's fragile hand and rubbed the top of it with his thumb. The warmth of her body caught in his throat. Not that her life was at risk, but to see her so frail, lying with a leg brace on a hospital bed in the poorly lit area of the far end of the ER. . .well, it made a man thankful for the small things in life. How was he going to say good-bye to this woman? She'd been a part of his life ever since he could remember. She was as important to him as his own grandparents—and just as bossy, possibly more so. He loved the old gal. "Get well, Freda, I'll see you in the morning," he whispered.

He turned. "Come on, Kayla. Let's get you home."

During the drive home, Warren filled Kayla in on all the calls he'd made. Who knew, who didn't, who probably did by now. She was grateful for all his help. He had told her earlier today he was a patient man. *That seems like days ago,* he thought. But every moment with Kayla brought him closer and closer to losing his patience. He wanted—no, he needed—to comfort her. She awoke the most primitive feelings inside him. The need to be a man, to protect the woman he loved. To protect the things she loved. But Freda and all of her needs far exceeded his ability. Only God could comfort and heal that.

There's a time appointed for each person to die. He firmly believed that. But when you saw people suffer, losing their minds to this horrible aging disease, how did that measure up with the "appointed" time? *Of course, God, You know a few things I don't, but still, I don't understand it, Lord.*

Kayla rested on his shoulder. From the gentle purr of her breathing, he knew she was asleep. As his truck left the pavement and pulled into her driveway, Kayla sat up. "You're almost home, Darling."

"Thanks, Warren. I don't know what I would have done without you." Kayla slid toward the passenger door.

"My pleasure. I'll visit Freda tomorrow."

"You don't have to."

"I know, but I want to. No, that's not true. I need to. She's been a part of my life for a very long time." Warren heard his voice catch.

Kayla opened the door and turned back toward him. The dim light of the cab accented the weariness in her green eyes. Her auburn tresses blanketed her shoulders. She reached out and took his hand. "I'm sorry, Warren. Of course, you'll want to see her."

Warren wrapped his fingers around her soft delicate ones. He loved touching this woman. "I love her, Kayla, as if she were my own grandmother."

"Her own grandchildren and great-grandchildren live so far away, it's hard for them to visit often. I'm sure she cherished her relationship with you just as much."

He simply nodded his agreement. Emotions coursed through his veins like a hailstorm close to harvest.

"Oh, Warren." Her voice brought him out of his thoughts. "Come here." She leaned toward him; he reached for her. Twice in one day he had allowed himself to be vulnerable to this woman. He was taking a risk showing her a piece of his heart. He only prayed she wouldn't trample on it.

Kayla's strong embrace wasn't the tender embrace of a lover, but rather an embrace of a person grieving over the loss of someone special. Freda hadn't died, at least not physically, but of the woman they knew, there was little left.

"Thanks, Kayla, I'm glad you understand."

"I'd be blind not to. Thanks for supporting me these past days and months. I don't think I could have held out as long as I have."

"You'll be placing her in a home?"

"I don't see many other options. I'll put her in temporarily. See if she recovers from the broken leg. But the doctor wasn't too encouraging on that score."

"No, he wasn't, I have to admit. But give it a day or two before you decide. Pray it through, okay?"

"Yeah, you're right. The middle of the night after a long emotional day isn't the best time to decide."

"No, it isn't. Take the few days she's in the hospital to explore your options. Talk with your father and any other member of your family that would want to help decide."

"You're right. I need to really pray and think this through. Not react to the exhaustion and guilt." Kayla leaned over and gave him a quick kiss on the cheek.

Warren grinned. "You missed."

Kayla chuckled. "Don't think so. Good night, Warren."

"Night, Kayla. I'll call you tomorrow."

"Okay." She slipped out of the cab and quickly made it to her front door.

He popped the truck into gear. "At least I got a kiss, Lord."

❧

The next morning came too soon for Warren. After his chores, he joined his folks for breakfast.

"How bad of a break is it, Son?" George reached for the jam.

"A fractured right femur. Due to her age and the Alzheimer's, they'll need to keep her in a wheelchair. There's no way she could handle crutches. Not to mention that brace is clear up to her hip."

"What's Kayla going to do?" his mother asked, setting herself down in her chair. "She can't take care of Freda when she's like that."

"She's looking into a nursing home and asked the doctor about some in-home nursing care." Warren scooped some hash browns onto his plate.

"But with a wheelchair? Is that place able to handle a wheelchair? There's steps going up into the house. I know Freda's sleeping downstairs, and Kayla, too, but still, can she maneuver a wheelchair in those small bedrooms?"

"You're so practical, Mom. I really don't know. Those are some of the issues that need to be discussed before she decides whether or not she can bring Freda home."

"I'm sure Kayla and her family will make the right decision." George chomped down on his toast covered with jam. "By the way, the fire department is saying the contractor has too many houses tied into that transformer. Appears someone was paid to look the other way."

"What's that going to mean for all those folks living in that development?" Warren asked.

"The power company needs to come in and build another transformer. But just who's going to pay for the work. . .now that's the question. Folks want the contractor to pick up the tab. The power company doesn't want to absorb the cost, and they're claiming they built the transformer according to the size and specifications the contractor gave them. Looks like the contractor was cutting costs, and folks are getting nervous."

"Another transformer shouldn't be a big deal." Warren put down his coffee. He needed the caffeine this morning, but he was thinking of catching a couple hours of sleep before lunch instead.

"Basically, it comes down to this. If the contractor cut corners on the electric, where else did he cut corners?"

"Ah, I gather folks in the development are pretty upset."

"Appears so. Some are even on the town council, and they are the ones with the power to grant future building contracts. Oh, and before you ask, it's the same guy who was looking to buy our place."

"Figures." Warren wiped his mouth with his napkin. "If you'll excuse me, folks, I need to make up for some of the lost sleep. I'm going to take a nap for a couple hours, then get to work."

"You do that, Son. What time was it when you got home— three?"

"Around there." It was closer to four, but his folks didn't need to know that. His father would try and do some of his work for him, and Warren didn't want his father having to take up his slack.

thirteen

Kayla held the cold rail of Freda's bed. Her parents were coming and would be staying at the farmhouse with her for a few days.

Freda's breathing was steady, but the doctors had her so sedated that she'd slept through Kayla's visit so far.

She reached out and held Freda's hand. Her skin was paper thin and yet warm. Freda's eyes fluttered open.

"Hi, Gram."

A smile creased across Freda's parched lips, the pupils of her eyes wide open and unfocused. Kayla stood beside her grandmother and brushed her gray hair from her face and continued to hold her hand. "How are you?"

"Where am I?"

"In a hospital. You broke your leg."

Freda lifted her head slightly, then tried to lift her legs. "Hurts like—"

"Yeah, I know, Gram. But it'll get better." But somehow Kayla didn't believe it would.

She'd been on the phone with nursing homes and in-home care agencies in the area all morning. With each call she felt defeat. Thankfully, her parents were going to investigate the various homes with her. Most would take Freda's social security payments until she sold the farm. But Kayla couldn't sell the farm until she obtained legal guardianship over her great-grandmother. When she had looked into that before, she discovered that the lawyers would get a huge cut on the sale of the house, and that much more would be taken away from her grandmother and the family's inheritance. No, there had to be a better way.

"Joann, who's looking after Mother?" Freda focused her gaze on Kayla.

"Mother is fine. Just relax and get better."

Freda was once again back to her youth. She was eighteen years old when her mother got sick and died. And Freda was the one who had to take care of her. For some reason, that event stuck in Freda's mind more than most other events. Kayla figured the death of Freda's mother, and the helplessness she felt not being able to make her mom well and whole, related to the helplessness Gram felt now.

Kayla knew the feeling, because she, too, felt it just as strong and real. She was helpless to heal Freda. The disease would take its toll, and eventually she'd pass on to her new life in Christ. As true as that reality was to Kayla, it still didn't stop the frustration she felt for a loved one suffering.

Father, I'm not sure I can handle this, she prayed silently.

"How soon can I attend classes?" Freda asked.

"Huh?" Kayla half heard her grandmother.

"When can I go back to college? I need to finish. Will you stay and take care of Mother?"

"Sure. Once you're up and around, you can go back." Kayla's mind spun. *College? When did Freda go to college? Did she? Or did she have to stop her education because of her mother?*

"Hello, Sweetheart," her father's voice called from the doorway.

"Dad, Mom, it's good to see you." Kayla held back the tears.

Her father stepped forward, firmly embracing her. "How is she?"

"She's been sleeping mostly, but she was just talking to me. Well, actually she's talking with her sister Joann about when her mother was ill and dying."

"Ah, a bittersweet memory." Her father slipped to Freda's bedside. "Hi, Gram," his voice boomed as it echoed through the room.

"Edwin?"

"No, Gram, I'm Charles."

"Charles? Do I know you?"

"Yes, but it's been a while since we've seen each other."

"Oh. Do you know Edwin?"

"Placate her, Dad. It works best," Kayla offered.

"Yes, Gram."

"Handsome man. He's asked me to marry him."

Charles chuckled, but his face reddened as tears built in his eyes. "Take him up on it, Freda. He's a good man."

"Well, I think I will. He's got the best set of shoulders I've ever seen on a man."

The room erupted in laughter.

"Hey, can I join this fun room?" Warren asked.

"Warren, come on in. These are my parents, Charles and Eleanor Brown."

"Hello, we've met before," Warren offered.

"Several times," Charles responded as Eleanor went up to Freda's bedside and whispered in her ear.

"Mom, the other ear. She can't hear a thing out of that one now."

"Oh, okay." Eleanor made her way to the other side of the bed.

Kayla glanced at Warren. "You look terrible."

"Gee, thanks." He pulled his Stetson off and held it over his heart. "I got about five hours sleep. How about yourself?"

"I managed five, too. I didn't get here until ten."

"Good. And you look great, by the way." Warren winked.

"It's nearly dinnertime. Should we all go grab something

to eat?" Charles suggested.

"I'll be happy to stay with Freda, while all of you go eat." Warren moved up to Freda's bedside and leaned over and kissed her cheek. "How's my favorite gal today?"

"Edwin?" She knitted her eyebrows.

Kayla looked at Warren. He was tall, but he didn't have Ed's shoulders. Kayla definitely understood Freda's confusion.

"No, Ma'am. I'm Warren, George's son."

"Oh, George, how nice to see you. How's your son?"

Warren grinned. "Just fine, Freda, just fine."

Kayla caught her father's glance. "Is she like this all the time?"

"Just about. Once in a while, she has a moment of clarity, but they are getting fewer. Sometimes it goes for days before we have one of those moments."

Charles gave a curt nod.

Kayla winced. There would be no arguing them into a nurse at the house, she feared.

"Warren, I'd like you to join us, if you'd like."

"Thanks for the kind offer, but I ate before I came. I can't stay all that long, and I'd like to visit with Freda for awhile."

"Very well. Eleanor, Kayla, let's go."

Kayla didn't want to leave. It wasn't that she couldn't use a break from being at Freda's bedside, but rather that she wanted to be with Warren.

At dinner, she explained to her parents what had been transpiring with Freda for the past week or so with the rapid daily deterioration. There was no question in her mind any longer: Freda had crossed the threshold from the middle stages to the final stages of Alzheimer's.

They discussed nursing homes. Some Kayla had eliminated simply from their phone responses, then pointed out the ones she was most interested in. She even got her parents to talk about an in-house nurse's aide.

"Kayla, did you find the will?" her father asked over a healthy slice of lemon meringue pie.

"Sorry, Dad. I meant to look for it, but I simply didn't have a chance."

"We'll find it at the house later," Eleanor interjected. "It isn't a problem, but with the nursing home issue coming up, we'll need to know."

૨ન

Warren kneaded the stiffness out of his neck as he steered his truck down the highway. Freda had slept through his visit, but he didn't regret his time spent with her. In the end, he knew it didn't matter to Freda, but it helped him in some small way. He thought he'd been prepared to let go of Freda, but the recent downward spiral and the injury all proved he wasn't ready.

A few cars sped past him. Warren looked down at the speedometer. "No wonder." He was going thirty miles per hour in a sixty-mile-an-hour zone. He pushed his foot harder on the accelerator, and the large V-8 engine hummed to life. He passed the turnoff to the new development and noticed the dimly lit houses. Were they trying to conserve power in the hopes of not blowing the transformer again?

A sign next to the development read "Future Homes by M. J. Construction." It appeared to have been plastered with mud balls. Warren headed into downtown Lakeland and stopped at Brian Jackson's store.

He priced some plywood and two-by-fours. If Freda were to come home, they'd need to build ramps for the wheelchair access. The toilet would need to be changed, as well as the tub removed and a shower installed with rail handles bolted into the wall. He pulled out a small spiral notepad and started his calculations.

As he turned down the aisle to the plumbing section, he saw Brian and Mack Jefferies in an animated discussion. Warren pushed himself down the row of sinks to the commodes. Finding a white porcelain handicap commode wasn't too difficult. Seeing there were no other options, he wrote the price for the toilet.

"What are you doing here?" Brian huffed as he marched toward Warren.

"Just pricing handicap bathroom necessities."

"Handicap?" Brian relaxed his stance.

"Yeah, some friends might need to install them in their home." For some reason, he wanted to protect Kayla from Brian's inquisition, and decided not to tell him who his friends might be. Not that Brian wouldn't guess.

"We can order whatever you need. There are catalogs over by the kitchen sinks and counters."

"Thanks." Warren headed to the next section after posting the price for a bathroom sink designed for a wheelchair.

Warren's cell phone rang.

"Hello."

"Warren, it's Mom. Where are you?"

"At Jackson's Supplies. What's up?

"You need to hurry to Kayla's. The police are there. Something's terribly wrong."

"Police? Kayla's? What's wrong?" Warren began to run through the aisle toward the front doors.

"I don't know, but Kayla's father is looking for you. Says you're the only one that can help."

"I'm on my way." Warren slid into the cab and turned the key in the ignition. *Police? Why could they possibly need to see Kayla? Something isn't right.*

Warren skidded around the curve, wheels screeching. "Slow down, old boy, or you'll never get there," he chastised himself.

His heart raced. His hands clutched the steering wheel tighter. "Oh, Lord, I haven't a clue what is going on. Please take control. Thanks."

⁂

"You can't be serious," Kayla snapped at the police officer.

"Afraid so, Miss. We need to question you about Freda's alleged fall." Kayla couldn't believe her ears or eyes. To see two police officers at her front door accusing her of possibly doing injury to Freda seemed surrealistic.

"Alleged? Are you implying that she didn't fall?" Kayla fought back the desire to scream at the taller of the two officers.

"We're only doing our job, Miss. Please, sit down. We need to ask you a few questions," the older and less fit of the officers suggested.

Her father returned to the living room. "I called my attorney. He said not to answer any questions until he arrives."

"When will that be, Sir?" the officer with a pencil-thin nose asked.

"He's hoping he can be here in three hours."

"Three hours." The short stocky officer plopped into his seat. "And my wife's making pot roast tonight."

"Look, Mr. Brown, these are just standard questions. The doctor at the hospital had to report the incident. He felt there was enough bruising on the outside of the leg to indicate she might have been hit."

"That's ludicrous. She simply fell getting out of bed."

"Yes, Miss, we have your report from the hospital."

"Then why are you here?" Kayla demanded.

The shorter officer took off his hat and placed it on the table. "Sit down, Ralph, and ease up." He turned to Kayla. "Would it be too much trouble to ask everyone to sit down and relax?"

Kayla shook her head from side to side. "No."

Charles escorted Eleanor to the table. Kayla sat in Gram's chair.

"Look—Kayla, right?" The older police officer took control of the situation.

"Yes," she calmly responded.

"Word around town is you've been taking great care of Freda. I don't doubt that. But we need to do our job. Unfortunately, the laws are such that if doctors don't report questionable circumstances, they are in danger of suffering heavy fines and even the loss of their licenses. Now, we do have a couple questions. They aren't a real big deal. If your lawyer is coming, we can wait. But I don't think it is necessary." The officer narrowed his gaze on his partner. "Town's been in an uproar about the transformer blowing across the lake from you. I'm afraid my partner here kinda came in here like a bull in a china closet." He gave a stern look at the man he called Ralph. "By the way, I'm Bill Masterson. This here is Ralph Dunbar."

"You said the doctor thought Gram had been struck in the leg?" Kayla asked.

"Yes, there was a contusion on the surface of her skin. Now that could have happened from her falling on something on the floor."

"I–I don't think there's anything on the floor. I haven't been in her room since I left with her to go to the hospital."

"May we have a look?" Officer Masterson asked.

Kayla looked at her father. Charles nodded. "Sure. I'll show you." She led them down the hall to Gram's back bedroom. Her room faced the lake, with a couple of windows overlooking the back field and the hills across the lake. The creak of the policemen's leather holsters made the only sound as they approached the room.

Kayla's palms lined with sweat. Images of Freda's crumpled

body on the carpet caused her to pause. Pieces of ripped open IV bottles, the plastic sleeves that carried the tubes and paper gauze littered the floor, left by the paramedics. Tears burned the edges of her eyes, but she refused to cry. She needed to be strong. She needed to face this as an adult. Why would anyone have accused her of beating her great-grandmother?

fourteen

Warren skidded to a halt on the pea stone driveway. The sight of a cruiser sitting outside Kayla's home made his heart tighten. He rushed out of the truck and through the front door. "Kayla?"

Charles and Eleanor stood in the hallway to the back bedrooms. They appeared surprised that he'd barged into the place, but then smiles grew on both their faces.

"She's in Freda's room."

Charles and Eleanor stepped aside and let him pass.

He eyed the two officers crouched down on the floor. "Kayla, what's the matter?"

"The doctor reported that it was possible Gram had suffered a blow to her leg, and that's why it broke."

"That's ridiculous. We were both in the dining room when it happened."

The officer named Ralph perked up his head. "You were here?"

"Yes, Sir. Kayla and I were saying good night when we heard the thump and moan. The two of us came running into the bedroom. And I stayed with Freda while Kayla called 911."

"Was anyone else here?"

"At the time of the accident, no. What's going on, Bill?" Warren reached his arm around Kayla's waist.

"Seems to me we've got an overprotective doctor. If you were here, you're a witness that Kayla didn't harm Freda."

"There's no way! Kayla breaks her back day in and day out caring for Freda. I don't know of another person who gives so lovingly to others."

"Your word's good with me," Bill said. "Would you mind coming to the station tomorrow and signing a statement?"

"With pleasure."

"Come on, Ralph. I've got a pot roast waiting for me at home."

"Just a second, Bill. Do you always keep her window open?" Ralph peered at the window.

"Most of the time. She prefers fresh air to air-conditioning."

"Did you know the screen's ripped at the bottom?" Ralph questioned. "How far to the ground is it from this sill?"

"I don't know, three feet, maybe four," Kayla guessed.

"Mind if I take a look?" Ralph asked.

"No."

Kayla shook. The idea of someone sneaking into the house and attacking Freda seemed really far-fetched. *Why would anyone want to harm her?*

"He's just being cautious, Honey," Warren assured her. "Relax. I'm sure nothing is out there."

Warren led her to the living room. Her parents moved slowly in front of them. It did seem odd that the femur was fractured though, but old folks' bones were brittle. Warren tightened his protective hold around Kayla.

The two officers worked their way to the back door of the house and departed quietly.

Charles cleared his throat. "Kayla, something's not right. Did you or Warren hear anything before Gram fell?"

"No, Daddy. We were sitting right here on the couch. . . talking." She hesitated, Warren noticed.

"Sir, earlier that day Freda had another paranoid episode. She said two men were after her money. Kayla thought it was the ushers collecting the offering during church."

"Who's to know what goes on in the mind of a patient with Alzheimer's?" Eleanor mused. "Personally, I think the police are just being overly cautious, and I didn't appreciate the way they barged in here accusing Kayla of beating Freda. Something ought to be done about that, Charles."

A cough from the kitchen doorway shifted their gazes to Bill. "Excuse me, folks. But there is evidence that someone may have tried breaking into Freda's room. Warren, Kayla, did the two of you hear anything strange that night?"

"Not a sound," Kayla offered.

"Were you watching TV perhaps? Listening to music?" Bill stepped into the living room and pulled a dining room chair with him.

"No, just talking," Kayla and Warren said in unison.

"Anything turn up missing recently, Kayla?"

"No, not that I can recall. But the house has been upside down for days. We just replaced the kitchen flooring." Kayla tightened her hold of Warren's hand.

Bill sat down and sighed. "Would you mind closing up Freda's room and not moving anything for the night? Tomorrow I'll send a detective to look around."

"With Gram in the hospital, we won't be here much. But why would anyone break in? The house is never locked. Wouldn't they just use the front or back doors?" Kayla asked.

"Probably just kids. Don't be alarmed, Kayla. I'm sure it's nothing." Bill got up from his chair and slid it back in its place under the table. "If you two will just come to the office and sign the statement, that should be the end of things."

"Okay." Kayla's voice quivered.

Charles stood up. "I'll want to read that statement before my daughter signs it."

"Of course. And she can add or take away anything that isn't her recollection of the evening's events."

Charles nodded. "I think we better get our suitcases before the sky is completely dark, Mother."

Eleanor stood and joined her husband.

"Good night, folks. Sorry for the trouble." Bill placed his blue police cap back on his head and held the door open for Charles and Eleanor.

The screen door slammed in its frame. Kayla turned into Warren's embrace. "I can't believe this is happening."

"Shh, Darling. Everything's going to be just fine. Thank the Lord I was here when she fell. Now there will be no more questions."

"Do you think someone actually assaulted Gram?" Kayla shivered in his arms. "Right here, in her own home, with us in the other room—is it possible?"

"No, Darling. I don't think it's possible. We would have heard something. No one is that quiet."

"I guess, but we were kinda focused on each other."

Warren grinned and wiggled his eyebrows. "Yeah, and I rather enjoyed it."

She whacked his chest. "Oh, you."

❧

Moments later, Kayla lifted her hand and tenderly pushed the velvety chocolate hair from his forehead. His dark brown eyes lit with golden specks focused on her own. Slowly his head descended toward hers.

"May I kiss you?" he whispered.

She blinked and rose to meet his lips. The kiss was so sweet and tender she melted deeper into his embrace.

The creak of the front door flitted into her ears, lodging someplace in her brain, the place where logic and reason performed. It meant something, but she couldn't pull away from Warren's kiss. She wrapped her arms around his neck.

He eased back.

She pulled him closer.

He eased back again.

She began to pull him back yet again.

Then the distinct sound of her father clearing his throat penetrated her fuzzy brain. He was in the room; she was being watched.

Kayla flung herself from Warren's embrace.

"So, someone could have come in last night and you two lovebirds wouldn't have heard a thing," Charles snapped.

"Charles," Eleanor reprimanded.

"No, Daddy, we weren't. . .we didn't. . .oh, phooey, no one believes anything I say anymore. What's the use." Kayla flopped onto the couch.

"Sir, for what it's worth, that was the first kiss Kayla and I've shared." Warren laid a protective hand on her shoulder.

"If that was a first kiss, you two better be careful with a second one." Eleanor cautioned.

Warren nodded.

Kayla's face flamed. How embarrassing could it get? She felt like she was sixteen, caught kissing her boyfriend on the front porch. Of course, Tommy's kiss hadn't been as heart-stopping as Warren's.

"Charles, we've all had quite the emotional past few days. Let's go upstairs, shower, and get ready for bed. I believe Kayla and Warren can handle their own company without our meddling."

Charles huffed and picked up their suitcases.

"I'm sorry to have put you in an embarrassing moment with your parents, Kayla. But I'm not sorry for kissing you." Warren knelt in front of her, tenderly massaging his thumb over the tops of her hands.

❧

The silence between them was comfortable. At last, Warren stirred. "Honey, I was at Jackson's Supplies when my mom called me on the cell phone."

"You have a cell phone?" She blinked.

"Yeah." Did she still see him as a country bumpkin? "But our family doesn't use it unless one of us is out of town or working far off on the farm." Warren shook off the question and continued. "As I was saying, I was at the store pricing the items needed to make the house handicap accessible. I'm sure tonight isn't a good time to discuss that option, but I wanted to have the figures ready for you and your folks if it is something you decide is a possible option. But, Darling, don't get me wrong here; if you don't have nursing staff helping you, there's no way you can take care of Freda in her present condition. It's just too much."

"I know. I'm resigning myself to the possibility that Gram's only alternative is a nursing home."

Warren lifted her chin so he could stare into those emerald eyes one more time. "It's late, your folks are going to want to talk, and I need some rest. I don't want to leave, but I really must."

"I don't want you to go, but that's purely selfish motives on my part."

"Darling, I like the sound of that." Warren grinned. "We need to talk, about us, but that will have to wait until decisions are made regarding Freda. That probably makes me the most foolish man in the state. But I love you, Kayla. I have for a very long time. I want to develop a relationship with you, but now is not the time."

Kayla's forehead creased.

"I mean, right now you're full of conflicting emotions, all circulating around your grandmother, her disease, your family, the pressures to sell the farm, everything. I want to wait until things have calmed down before we pursue our relationship. As much as I want to take you into my arms right now, I also believe we need to take a step back and pray, seek the Lord, and trust Him for our future."

Kayla's soft fingers traced the shadow of his beard to the cleft in his chin. "I hear what you're saying, but as much as you're a patient man, I'm an impatient woman. And once I see what I want, I have a mind to go for it."

Warren chuckled. If that kiss was a taste of her "going for it," he was in trouble. "Oh, Darling, have mercy."

"I will pray, Warren. And you're right, my life is in a tailspin. And I'm not the kind of woman to kiss and want to be married tomorrow. Although the prospect has some interesting possibilities," she said with a smirk.

"Kayla." Warren sighed.

"The fact is, you're right."

"Thank you, I think." Warren sat down on the carpet in front of her, holding her hands in his. She was incredible, but he was only beginning to see her depth.

They talked for another fifteen minutes about the next few days' plans. He had to go to the southern field and finish his testing there.

"We've a lot to learn about each other." She stood and helped pull him up.

"Yes, we need time. Do you have the courage to pursue a relationship, knowing we both feel led in different directions in terms of careers?"

"If we take it one step at a time, I think I can muster enough courage."

"No, Kayla. Give it to God. He'll give you the courage regarding your grandmother and us. Stop doing it in your own strength and trust Him."

"What do you mean, doing it in my own strength? I pray. I ask for His help with Gram." Her voice raised an octave.

"Yeah, but do you allow Him to do it?" Warren challenged.

"Of course, I—"

Warren held his finger to her lips. "Shh, Darling, don't answer me. Pray. I think you'll find most of the time you've been trusting yourself and no one else, not even God."

"Warren, why?" Tears filled her eyes.

He pulled her into his chest. "Honey, I'm sorry. I didn't mean to hurt you. I might be wrong. But pray about this. And ask yourself why in the past ten months you've only once, ten days ago, in fact, allowed yourself some personal time? Why have you been caring for her twenty-four/seven?"

He could feel her anger mount as her back stiffened in his arms. He kissed the top of her head. His lips slid to her ears, and he whispered, "I've been praying for awhile about this. If I'm wrong, I apologize. I only ask you to pray."

He released her then and left her smoldering. He'd blown it. He'd gone too far, too soon again. *Father, comfort her.*

fifteen

"How dare he?" Kayla stomped into her bedroom. On little rest, she'd spent the day at the hospital, had dinner with her folks, come home to be questioned by the police, kissed Warren. . .she gently touched her lips. . .and ended up getting insulted by the man. He was right about one thing: Her emotions were running amok.

How could she have kissed him with such abandonment? How could she, with her parents just feet away? Perhaps the kiss was just a connection with stability. If nothing else, Warren Robinson was a very stable man.

She stood in front of her mirror and brushed out her hair. He said he loved her. The brush paused midstroke. Did she love him? Kayla continued the long strokes through her hair. Attracted, she was definitely attracted.

But love? She sunk the brush deep into her auburn waves.

Ten months you've known this man. Why now? Why do you find yourself so drawn to him? She interrogated the image in the mirror, pointing her brush at the paled reflection.

"And just who does he think he is, trying to tell me I'm caring for Gram in my own strength? I've prayed. I've trusted God." She let a pent-up growl escape her lips.

"Perhaps because he cares." Her mom's tender words caused Kayla to turn and face her. "Want to talk about it?"

"No. . . Yes. . . I don't know."

Eleanor chuckled and came up beside her. She took the brush from Kayla's hand and brushed her hair. "When did you start having feelings for Warren?"

"Just the past week or so. He's so sweet with Gram. He's tender, thoughtful, kind, and so different from another man I recently spent time with."

"Oh, and who is he, Dear?" Eleanor continued to brush.

"His name is Brian Jackson. But it seems like he's looking for an ornament to attach to his arm at parties. Once I got this shiner, he broke our date, saying he couldn't take me to this party because others would think he was responsible for it."

"I see. And how was he with Gram?"

"Ignored her. Told me to put her in a home, sell the place. I've since learned he's working side by side with the man trying to buy all the farms adjacent to the lake."

Eleanor stopped brushing and looked into Kayla's reflected eyes in the mirror. "If you feel you're being used, you probably were."

"Yeah, but why? What difference does it make if Gram's land is sold or remains as a farm?"

"I'm not sure, but your father's been getting quite a few calls of interest about the property lately. He's determined to find Freda's will and see if that has some clue as to why there's all this sudden interest."

"I don't know, Mom. The contractor, Mack Jefferies, was saying he wanted to put a school and some public buildings on the farm, and condos on the waterfront property."

"Big plans. Is the man intending to rebuild the entire town?"

"I don't know, didn't take the time to ask. He did mention that, with today's commuters, he's hoping to make Lakeland a bedroom community."

"But the city is over an hour away."

"Right, but he said folks travel that and more, and many work out of their homes and only go into the office once in a while."

"I suppose that's true. But your father says the man is cheap, really lowballed the offer for the farm. He's been going up in increments of $20,000 every time he calls when your father doesn't return his messages. Charles said that he received a call from your aunt Phyllis the other day, and that Mr. Jefferies also contacted her."

"He seems anxious. Warren's father's been made an offer, too, but I believe he's only had one contact with him."

Eleanor put the brush down on the dresser. "I'm nervous that someone would try and break into the house, Kayla. Something isn't right."

"I'm not too pleased to hear that myself. It certainly doesn't make sense, since the house is never locked." Kayla turned around and faced her mother.

"Think maybe you ought to start locking it?" Eleanor raised her right eyebrow.

"Yeah, but I don't have a clue where keys for the locks might be, and we'd probably have to oil all the locks in order for them to work."

Eleanor chuckled. "I imagine so. Come, your father is waiting for us."

❧

The next day Warren tried to let the horseback ride to the southern section calm his haggard nerves. Kayla had kissed him. She'd even indicated she might be out to pursue him. Such a difference in two weeks time. What had changed?

The gentle breeze stirred the tall grass. From up on his horse he could see a fair distance. The cows needed to be moved, and the ground needed to rest. He had already scattered various grass seeds to feed the cows. They'd done their job. The real test would be next year when he planted.

In the distance, he saw Timothy Daniels heading his way. He'd meant to spread the word at church last Sunday that the boy was looking for odd jobs, but Warren had forgotten. The whine of the teen's dirt bike perked up the cows' ears, but they continued to munch on their afternoon meal. His horse bayed. Warren rubbed the animal's neck. "It's okay, Boy."

Timothy cut his bike engine and waved. "Hey, Warren, checking on the soil again?"

"Nope, just getting some ideas and perspective. What brings you out here?" The fact that Tim had no problem riding his dirt bike on his property bothered him a tad.

"Was looking for you. Your folks said you'd be out here."

Okay, so maybe he had a reason to be on his land. Warren's previous concern eased. "What can I do for you?"

"Mr. Jackson said you were looking to do some construction for someone, and he thought you could possibly use a hand." Tim placed his hands on his hips.

Warren let a rumble of laughter rise in his throat. Timothy was working hard to earn the money he wanted for that computer. "I might be, but I'm volunteering again, and I'm not sure I can afford to hire you."

"Yeah, you paid me real well for the other night. I was hoping you might need a hand. But if you're not getting paid, I wouldn't want you to fork over the cash again. I've been getting some odd jobs. Mr. Jackson set me up with Mack Jefferies. He's needing errands and odd jobs run all the time. I've earned another fifty. Jefferies don't pay as well as you, though."

Warren stood in his saddle, looped his leg around, and dismounted. "Freda fell and broke her leg."

"Yeah, I heard. Word is they even sent the police out."

Does everything get repeated in this town? "False alarm. I was there when Freda fell."

"Wouldn't believe Kayla would whack Freda. That's just dumb." Tim removed his helmet and placed it on top of the seat of his dirt bike. "I kinda figured you were going to build for Freda, but I was hoping you'd be paid."

"Afraid not, and we're not even sure if she's coming home.

She may have to go to a nursing home."

"Freda would hate that." Tim straddled his bike.

"So would a lot of us. So, what kind of odd jobs have you been getting?"

"Mostly errands, running envelopes to different people. Stuff Mack wants in the hands of folks, ASAP. Says if he mailed it, they wouldn't get it till the next day."

"True."

"I was hoping he'd hire me to work on his construction crew. With all the houses he's building, there's plenty of work."

Warren nodded.

"Trouble is, I'm only fourteen. He said his insurance would skyrocket. So he's giving me little things to do."

"Sounds great. I'm glad you're finding the jobs to put the money away for a computer."

"Me, too, but Dad says I ought to put the money toward college. But if I had the computer, I could earn money doing graphic designs and stuff. He just doesn't get it."

"Computers weren't a big deal when your dad went to school. They just did simple data functions back then. It's hard for him to picture the difference, I imagine."

"Probably. I saw an old TV show once, *Superman,* I think. You know, the black-and-white one?"

Warren nodded.

"Really bad special effects." Timothy shook his head. "There's this scene when Superman's saving a computer. He brings out this huge tube, must have been around eighteen inches, with a six- to eight-inch diameter, and says something about how amazing it was that this tube held 40 kilobytes of information. Do you know how small that is today?"

"Amazing." Warren quickly did the math. "So it would take twenty-five of those tubes to hold what's on a diskette today."

"Yeah. Blows your mind, doesn't it? When the show was

filmed, that was cutting-edge stuff. Of course, it was nearly fifty years ago, back in the dark ages."

Warren chuckled. "Just remember, your dad was born in those dark ages."

"Don't remind me. He's ancient."

"I reckon so." Warren closed the gap between them. "Sorry I can't give you another job right now."

"No problem. Mack Jefferies is keeping me busy. Takes more time but it's steady."

"Glad to hear it. I need to get back to work. Take care." Warren mounted his horse. The creak of the leather saddle along with the smell of the horse and leather brought him back to simpler times. Times before Kayla.

Tim put on his helmet and kick-started the dirt bike. He waved, then twisted his wrist, giving the machine gas, and popped it into gear with his foot. He was off. The whine of the engine diminished as the distance increased.

Will I be building the handicap access for Freda? Warren wondered. He flicked the reins and nudged the horse with his knees. On the other hand, Warren had forced Kayla to look at herself and whether or not she was caring for Freda in her own strength. He winced at the memory.

"Why do I keep pushing her, Lord? Why can't we just take this slow, one step at a time?"

In the sky a sparrow floated on the gentle wind currents. It circled toward the small herd of cattle and flew back toward the lake.

"Trust Me."

The words seared his heart, and a wry grin creased his face. "Okay, Lord, I get Your point. I'll trust You to work with Kayla, just like she needs to trust You with Freda."

❧

"I found it!" Charles exclaimed.

Her father waved a blue tri-folded document through the air. They'd been searching for hours. Gram had always claimed her will was in her desk, but that proved to not be the case. They had scoured through boxes, closets, dresser drawers, any nook and cranny they thought she might possibly have placed it.

"Where'd you find it?"

"You'll never believe this." Charles brushed his long white hair across his bald spot.

Eleanor put her hands on her hips, demanding. "Charles, forget the suspense, just tell us."

"She taped it to the back side of her nightstand."

"What on earth for?" Eleanor inquired.

"I think I know." Kayla went up beside the nightstand and traced her father's initials he had carved in there years ago. "Remember this, Daddy?"

Charles groaned. "How could I ever forget? Gram reminded me of it many times after Jeremy had done the same to the dining room table."

The laughter bubbled in Kayla's throat. "She told me. Last week, in fact. I bet she knew after she was gone you'd remember the nightstand. She certainly knew you would be the executor of the will."

"She did have a way of putting you in your place." Her dad's eyes were wet.

Her mom slid her arm around Charles's waist and held him close. "She's not gone yet, Charles. Perhaps you'll get one of those special moments with her that Kayla says she still has."

He patted her hand. "I'd like that."

For a moment, the room filled with memories and the overwhelming awareness that Freda's time with her family was coming to an end. *Even if she has a few more years physically,* Kayla reasoned, *Freda is nearly gone.*

"Well, we've looked for that for hours. Let's see what it says."

Her mom stepped toward the hall leading out of Freda's room.

They sat around the table. Charles opened the will and began to read: "I, Freda Irene Brown, being of sound mind. . ." Her father's voice cracked.

"She was then, Dad." Kayla smiled.

"Yeah, she was then." Charles cleared his throat and continued, "On this date of May fifth, nineteen hundred and ninety-seven. . ."

Charles continued to read. "She's got more land here than I thought."

Kayla and her mom leaned closer. "Seems she's giving anyone in the family, blood relative, that is, the property for free, but they can only use it for farming. They can't parcel it up and sell it. They can rent the land like she's been doing with other farmers. But they can't sell it. She's also stipulated that if no one in the family wants the land, it is to be sold to a farmer, a Mr. Warren Robinson."

"Warren?" *Gram's selling the land to Warren?* She was determined that the land stay as farmland, and Warren was a good choice. He had the same convictions about farming and the need for farms as Freda.

"Apparently." Charles grinned. "She also states that he's to purchase the land for a fair market value for farmland at the time it becomes available. But he's not to pay higher than $200,000."

"Wow, that's nothing compared to what Mack Jefferies is offering. She was a determined old lady, wasn't she?"

Charles guffawed. "Yup. She told me many times it was to remain a farm, and that she'd take the appropriate steps to make certain it did."

Eleanor sat back in her chair. "But if Warren's to get the property, and the land can't be used for anything but farming, why all the fuss?"

sixteen

"She what?" Warren couldn't believe Kayla's words. She'd called and asked him to come over this morning for breakfast. Sitting on the table was Freda's will. His hands shook as he lifted the legal parchment. "I can't believe she did this."

"First, the family has to decide if anyone wants to be a farmer."

"I understand."

"Warren." Kayla cupped his hand with hers. "Gram loves you, and I think she respected the man you are, the farmer you want to be. You and she have very similar ideas about farming."

"I imagine so. We talked often enough about it over the years." Warren's gaze flitted back and forth from the will to Kayla. "Doesn't this bother you, your parents? The other members of your family?"

"I don't think so. Remember, we were raised by her, more or less. We picked up her ideals—but we all had our own dreams and desires for careers. Gram encouraged that. But she was also equally committed to the farm, to the dream she and Gramps had shared."

Warren rubbed a hand over the faint stubble of overnight growth. He normally didn't shave until after chores and breakfast. "She told me once, back a few years, after I came home from college, that she wanted to sell me the place. I guess that's when I started planning and dreaming of one day being able to buy it."

"Looks like she made sure you could. There was a note to

my dad that she had placed within the will. Basically, she explained her reasons, the things that can't get stated in the will. She also said the house and barns would go to you when you purchased the farm, but any furniture or other contents was for the family to split up and divide among ourselves."

Kayla traced her finger up Warren's forearm. He dropped the will and captured her hands with his own. "I've missed you, Darling."

"I missed you, too." Kayla's eyes drifted down to the floor.

He wanted to pull her into his arms; he wanted to kiss her. But he promised himself he would be patient and wait. "I didn't know Freda owned this many acres. Did your father find the property map?"

"No, and that's the strangest thing. No one knew there was this much land, and yet no one is sure where those other acres are."

"You can go to the county records. They'll have it on file," Warren offered.

"Dad's there this morning. We still can't figure out why there's all this fuss about wanting to buy her land. Granted, if Mack Jefferies looked at county records he might know how many acres Freda owns, but still it doesn't make sense."

"No, I guess it doesn't." Warren gazed at the green discoloration around her eye. The bruise was nearly faded.

"What?"

Warren felt the heat rise on his neck. "Oh, I was just noticing how much the bruise faded."

Kayla groaned. "It's taken forever. I had more folks staring at me in the hospital, figuring I was a patient, I guess. Brian was right about one thing: If he'd taken me out Friday night, everyone would have thought he'd clobbered me."

Warren released her hands, reacting to the mere mention of Brian's name. He needed to get over this jealousy.

"Warren?" she questioned. "You know, I'm not interested in Brian."

He nodded. What could he say? *Sure, I know, but I'm still jealous of the man. He's got the looks and build of a Mr. Universe.* Whereas he himself was little more than a gangly skeleton—long, tall, and enough muscles to hold it together under a nondescript layer of skin.

"Warren? Talk to me."

"Not much to say. I know you aren't interested in him."

"But?" Kayla pushed.

"I've seen the men in your family, Kayla. I don't quite measure up, physically, that is. Not like Brian does."

"Oh, so you think I'm like Gram, attracted to men with beefy pecs and shoulders?"

"Freda said that?"

Kayla's eyes danced with laughter. "Yeah, the other day in the hospital. Remember when you walked in on us and we were all laughing?"

Warren nodded his head slowly. "Yes."

"Well, Gram had just expressed how Gramps had great shoulders, best she'd ever seen on a man." Kayla giggled. "It was so cute. She was back in time, around the time that she and Gramps began dating, I think."

"Ah."

Kayla grew serious. "Tell me something. Do I relax when I'm in your arms?" She grasped his hand and held it tightly, her green eyes penetrating his defenses.

What could he say? "Yeah."

"I can't believe I'm going to say this, but here it goes. Warren, you're not like any other man I've ever known. Yes, you're not built like my father or my brother or Brian. But when I'm in your arms, I feel complete. You calm me. And your love and concern for other people is so genuine. Look

what you've done for Timothy Daniels. And why?" She
paused and continued. "You didn't have to. But you reached
out because you believed God wanted you to. But you went
above and beyond. You paid the boy out of your own pocket,
just to help give him a sense of accomplishment. That type of
behavior, Warren Robinson, is what attracts me to you."

Forget patience. He pulled her into his embrace and kissed
her. She hadn't exactly declared her love, but she had certainly admitted her attraction. And it went beyond physical
appearance. It went to the heart of who he was as a man.
"Goodness, Woman, you're beautiful. Inside and out."

❧

Kayla's eyes fluttered open. She was trying to focus after one
of Warren's kisses. The word "beautiful" spiraled down her
senses, sinking deep into her heart. "So are you, Warren.
Despite what you might think about yourself. You are a handsome man. Oh, sure, Hollywood won't be knocking down
your door, but I wouldn't want them to. I—"

She stopped short of confessing how jealous she would
be, how glad that he was hers and hers alone. Because the
fact was, he wasn't. They were attracted, but was there a
future between them? What about her career? She'd put it
on hold for Freda. Was she supposed to put it on hold for a
husband, too?

"What?" he asked, pulling her back into his embrace.

"I'm just glad Hollywood isn't knocking down your door."

Warren lifted her chin with his forefinger and held it with
his thumb. She lazily embraced his shoulders. She needed to
break the tension that was between them. Good tension, but
tension, nonetheless. Otherwise, she would put her life on the
back burner without having taken the time to seek the Lord;
she didn't want to react simply on impulse.

She kneaded his shoulders with her fingers. "Hmm, feels

like you have shoulders to me." She wiggled her eyebrows.

"Ya think?"

༈

After Warren left, Kayla continued to ponder their relationship. She would definitely need to pray. Her attraction to him grew daily. Could she put aside her ambitions and marry a farmer? With a sigh, Kayla walked out to the garden and put on old cotton gloves.

Her parents were leaving today after visiting with Gram. The land search at the county office would take some more digging. On the surface, it appeared that Gram owned the lake, which didn't make sense. The problem was that she and her husband had bought the land back in the late twenties, just before the Depression. It was Kayla's job to search for the original land purchase and corresponding map, if there was one. But as it appeared now, the land under the lake belonged to Gram—but one can't own the water, can they?

She knew her father believed that maybe somewhere in the attic there might be some files, possibly some clues as to whether or not the lake was on the property when they bought the land. It seemed to him that possibly his grandparents allowed the lake to be constructed on their land, but that the water would be free and available to all the farmers, with no exclusive rights to the water.

It made sense, knowing Gram and how she felt about the community and the cooperation of the farmers working together. But why would that interest the folks wanting to buy Gram's land today?

Still, the questions remained. No answers, just more questions. And would something that happened back in the late twenties when they had purchased the land still be binding today?

For days, she'd neglected the garden, but now Kayla pulled

weeds with a renewed vigor. Her thoughts shifted to Gram, who was to be transported to a nursing home temporarily for further evaluation.

The family had decided they would pool their resources and provide for sixteen hours a day of private-duty nurses. Warren would oversee altering the house, and the money to pay for it would come from one of Freda's hidden CD accounts— something else the will had revealed.

Kayla's thoughts turned next to her Sunday school class. The mustard plants the children had planted nearly two weeks ago now stood inches tall and halfway through their cycle from seed to seed. Leaves were sprouting and tiny buds could be seen at the end of each stem. *In fertile soil the seeds grow—and they grow well and quickly, like our love for our Heavenly Father,* Kayla mused.

And like her love for Warren. It, too, was growing quickly and deeply.

Her mind flickered back to memories of her great-grandmother and the stories she'd told about her love for Ed, and how fast that relationship had grown.

"Father, are you developing that with Warren and me?" she prayed. Glancing over to where a small mound of weeds had gathered, she turned to pluck them up. Reds, oranges, and yellows painted the evening sky as the sun lowered over the horizon.

❧

As the weeks went by after Freda's accident, Kayla's days were different. She visited Freda every day, learning about bedsores and how to prevent them. Today, Kayla took a deep breath as she entered Freda's room.

"Hi, Gram," she cheerfully called.

Freda examined her. Clearly, she didn't recognize her again. It had been like this for the past week. Kayla sighed. She suspected Freda forgot her more often now that they were no longer sharing a home. The remodeling of the house was nearly finished, but she still couldn't take her great-grandmother home. Although Freda's leg was healing, the brace needed to remain for several more weeks.

Kayla leaned down and kissed Freda, then placed the fresh bouquet of purple and pink irises in her lap. "I thought you might like these, Gram."

Freda reached for the flowers and pulled them to her nose. "They don't smell?"

Kayla sniffed them; their fragrance was rich and sweet, but obviously Freda's sense of smell had left her. "Sorry. They're still pretty, aren't they?"

"Put them over there, Ann," Freda ordered, pointing to the nightstand beside her bed.

Ann? That was a new name, not even a family name. Perhaps one of the staff members was named Ann—or was she thinking of Warren's mother?

"How are you today?"

"Miserable," Freda pouted. "No one loves me. No one ever comes to visit me. I want to go home."

That was a hard pill to swallow, since Kayla had been here every day since Freda's accident. She had been piling the miles on her car just to come and see her every day. But Kayla shook off the words, knowing that another part of the disease had reared its ugly head. "I know, Gram. You can go home soon, I promise. Warren almost has the work done."

As if on cue, he walked through the doorway. "How's to-morrow sound?"

"Really?" Kayla's heart lightened.

"Yeah, I called in some favors. The place will be done by the time we get there tonight."

"Oh, Warren, that will be wonderful. I need to tell the staff.

I need to call the home health care. Oh, dear, there's so much I need to do."

Warren wrinkled his eyebrows and narrowed his gaze.

"Oh, all right, I'll pray and ask the Lord to lead me, and I'll stop long enough to listen. How's that?"

Warren's grin brightened. "Better, much better."

Kayla stuck her tongue out at him and scrunched her nose. He'd been right about her not trusting the Lord. She'd been trying to care for Freda in her own strength and not allowing the Lord to use others.

"Gram, Warren says you're coming home tomorrow."

Tears filled Freda's dark blue eyes. "Home?" she asked.

seventeen

Freda sat lethargically in the back of the medical van Kayla had to rent to bring her home. The nursing home had given her some additional medication to help with the transition. In Kayla's mind, they had just drugged up her grandmother so she wasn't aware of anything. Of course, the drugs would make her calmer. But Kayla had hoped to see a glimmer of excitement back in her great-grandmother's eyes. In the end, when they rolled her into the house, up the new walkway Warren had installed, Freda was barely aware of where she was.

Had they made the right decision to bring her home? *Tomorrow, things will be different,* Kayla hoped.

After the attendants left, she got Freda a cup of caffeinated coffee. *The woman needs some life back in her,* she justified.

"Here, Gram, have some coffee, black with cream, just the way you like it."

The unfocused, murky blue eyes looked up at her. Kayla's heart skipped a beat. "You're home now, Gram."

Freda's hand trembled as she raised the bone china cup to her lips.

"Thank you." Her throaty voice cracked.

"You're welcome, Gram. What would you like for lunch?"

"Nothing."

Freda always had a tremendous appetite and had always been in good shape. But a potbelly was starting to emerge. Lack of walking, Kayla presumed.

They sat in silence while Freda drank her coffee. Did Kayla dare give her another cup? Perhaps later with her lunch. *Father,*

I'm so lost. I don't know what to do, she silently cried out.

"Move her."

Oh, dear. Kayla had forgotten to shift her. The old woman had been in the wheelchair in the same position since departing the hospital, and who knows how long she'd been sitting in there before she arrived. Bedsores. . .yes, Kayla would have to watch for them.

A knock at the door startled Kayla. She left Freda and answered the door.

A woman in her fifties, with salt-and-pepper hair and a huge smile, greeted Kayla. "Ms. Brown?"

"Yes."

"I'm Jean Grist. I'm your private-duty nurse."

Kayla swung the door open for her. "Come in. We just arrived less than an hour ago."

"I came by earlier but you weren't here, so I went into town for a couple things, then came back." Jean leaned against Gram's favorite sitting chair. "You must be Freda." Jean walked up to her and pumped her hand.

Kayla smiled when the woman shouted her greeting. Clearly, Jean had read the report and knew Gram was hard-of-hearing. She even leaned into her left ear, the one that heard the best.

"I'm sorry we ran late. The nursing home had some more paperwork for me to sign when we left."

Jean rolled her eyes. "Don't they always? How long has she been sitting in this chair?"

"The entire trip and since. I was just about to adjust her. You'll see we've rented the flowing air seat cushion for her chair, and I've put one on her bed as well as the couch. I don't want her sitting only in her chair."

"Good. That will help reduce the possibility of bedsores. Coffee, huh?"

"She loves coffee." Kayla plastered a fake smile on her face. While it was true Gram loved coffee, it was also true she didn't need too much caffeine in her diet. Kayla had long ago decided, however, that her grandmother needed some joy in her life. If it shortened her days on the earth because she was drinking caffeine, so be it. She knew Freda didn't mind dying and meeting her Maker face-to-face.

"Mind if I have a cup?" Jean winked.

Kayla decided she liked this woman. "No problem. Why don't we set Gram on the couch and then I'll get you a cup?"

"Sure sounds like a good idea to me." Jean turned to Freda and raised her voice. "We're going to put you on the couch. Get you more comfortable."

Freda nodded.

Kayla was grateful for the therapist in the nursing home who had showed her how to lift someone from a wheelchair.

With Freda situated, Jean pulled out a notebook and sat down at the table. Kayla poured a cup a coffee for her and brought out the cream and sugar.

"Thanks, black is fine for me. Okay, I've got some more forms. I know, I know. I hate them as much as anyone, but there'll be four of us coming to take care of your grandmother. I'll be working mornings to afternoon, Bonnie will be coming in the afternoons to evening. Then you'll have the weekend staff of Dick and Jane."

"Dick and Jane?" Kayla chuckled.

"Yeah, they hear it all the time. Folks my age learned to read with Dick and Jane."

They worked over the forms and enjoyed the rest of the time together. Kayla showed her around the house, and Jean filled her in on what a private-duty nurse does and does not do. They weren't maids, but they would help Kayla with something if she needed it.

When Bonnie arrived in the afternoon, she found she enjoyed the much younger nurse as much as she enjoyed Jean, even though their personalities were as different as night and day. While Jean was outgoing, Bonnie was reserved and quiet. But both took the responsibility of caring for Freda's needs with enthusiasm.

☙

"Hey, Darlin', how'd it go today?" Warren stepped into the kitchen. He'd given up knocking on the door long ago.

"Really well. They drugged Gram for the transition, but I gave her a cup of coffee when we got home. Seemed to perk her up a bit. The private-duty nurses are great. You'll love them."

"Not nearly as much as you, my love." Warren captured her in his embrace.

"Just remember that when you see Bonnie," she teased.

"Oh?" Warren wiggled his eyebrows.

"She's young, attractive. You'll like her."

"Where is she? Or has she left already?" Warren craned his head to look into the living room.

"Oh, stop that. She's in the bedroom getting Gram settled for the night."

"Don't they know Freda likes to watch her merry-go-round show?" He stepped out of their embrace and held her hands, kneading the tops of them with his thumbs.

"Yeah, we moved my college television into her bedroom."

"Okay, so how's Freda doing back at home?"

"She's not really responded yet. Jean, she's the nurse who came first thing this morning, called Gram's doctor here in town to see if she could reduce the psyche meds. They had her on so many at the nursing home."

"I think they needed that many at the home to keep her calm. She doesn't like being strapped down. And while they didn't strap her down literally, that broken leg sure does keep her immobile."

"So, are you up for searching the attic again?"

"No, but I will. Just once, I'd like to take you out, Kayla. You know, go on a real date."

"You mean you don't like coming over here every day just to help out?" she teased.

"You know better than that. But I would like to take you out and get you away from here. Just once, I'd like to show you how I, the man who loves you, would treat a woman."

"Hmm, sounds heavenly, but—"

"I know, I know, but you can't blame a man for wanting to spoil his lady."

"Keep it up, Buster, and I'll find a way. I could use a night on the town." Kayla leaned into him and gave him a quick peck on the lips.

"Excuse me, I didn't mean to interrupt." A woman with long blond hair braided in the back stood in the kitchen doorway.

"Bonnie, I presume."

"Yes, Mr. Brown."

Kayla giggled. "Bonnie, this is Warren Robinson. He lives next door."

"Oh, sorry, I just assumed." A pale blush rose on the lightly tanned cheeks. Warren had to admit, Bonnie was a good-looking woman. But compared to Kayla she was a pale wallflower.

Warren removed his Stetson and brushed out his hair with his fingers, then placed an arm across Kayla's shoulders. "So, how's Freda?" he asked.

"I think she's becoming more aware of her surroundings," Bonnie offered, and poured herself another cup of coffee from the coffeemaker.

"Think I'll go visit Freda before we start on the attic, okay?"

"Sure. I've got some leftover chicken potpie, if you think you'll be hungry later."

Warren had been trying to place the wonderful aroma when he came in. "You know me. I'm always in the mood for some good food."

"I know you, all right. You eat like a horse and don't gain a pound. Did God give you hollow legs or something?"

"Or something." He winked. "Pleasure to meet you, Bonnie. But I must be going, Freda awaits."

He'd only seen Freda a few times over the past couple weeks. Working on the house, getting it ready for her, had taken every minute of his spare time. Thankfully, Kayla and he always shared a few quiet moments before he went home each evening. But there was no doubt about it: The past month was probably the most sleep-deprived month in his entire life. And that included finals at college.

"Hi, Freda. How's my favorite girl?"

Freda's eyes blinked. "Warren?"

Warren's grin broadened. She knew him! How long had it been? Weeks. "Yes, Freda, it's me, Warren. How's the leg?"

"Stiff."

Warren chuckled. "Yeah, a brace on it kinda makes it that way. I'm glad you're home, Freda."

"Me, too. Don't like those hospitals none. Always poking and prodding."

"Yeah, I don't fancy those nightgowns with the slit up the backside." Warren placed his hand on hers. "I saw the will, Freda. You shouldn't have."

Freda's eyes darted back and forth. Had he lost her again? He wanted to thank her just once when she knew who he was and who she was.

She reached her fingers up to his cheek. Her hand was so

soft and fragile. "I know you'll take care of the land."

Warren swallowed hard. "Yes, Ma'am, you know I will."

She patted him on his cheek. "Don't forget, you'll control the water. Ed saw to it that the town wouldn't ever charge the farmers for water. Gave up quite a parcel of land, but them rights will belong to you. I know you'll do right by the other farms."

Warren nodded his head. She had to be talking about the land under the lake, but how did that keep the water rights for the farmers? "Where's the document, Freda?"

"The bank."

"The bank? We've been through the safe-deposit box. It's not in there," Kayla interjected as she came into the room. "Gram, is there another bank?"

"Only one in Lakeland." Freda's eyes caught the television screen. Her smile lifted the wrinkles on the corners of her cheeks. "My show," she beamed.

Warren released Freda's hand and stepped back to join Kayla. "The bank," he whispered.

"Trust me, Warren. We've gone through every legal document. There's no other bank, and what was in the safe-deposit box is now in my father's. It's simply not there."

"Did you hear that Ed did something regarding the water?"

"Yeah, we need to find it, Warren." Kayla smiled. "I'm glad she had a moment with you. Those times are so special, aren't they?"

"Yes, very. I got to thank her for selling me the farm."

Kayla grinned. "You do realize if I or any one of my relatives decide to live here, you won't be able to buy the farm?"

"Has someone expressed interest?"

"Only one."

Warren took in a deep breath and let it out slowly. For weeks, he'd been drawing up plans for Freda's land. He'd even talked with the bank about getting the loan to buy the farm. He had enough for the down payment, and he was certain he could afford the mortgage. His father always said, though, "Don't count your chickens before they hatch." Guess he hadn't been listening to that age-old wisdom. "I'll help him or her any way I can."

"You would do that, wouldn't you?" Kayla's green eyes darkened. She placed her hand into his and led him out of Freda's room. "Warren, what if there was a way you could have the land and not have to pay a penny for it?"

❧

"What are you talking about?" Kayla felt the tug on her arm as he stopped dead in his tracks.

"I've been thinking about something Mack Jefferies said."

"The contractor?"

"Yeah." Kayla held back her grin and tried to maintain a deadpan expression.

"You're not making sense, Darlin'. What does Mack Jefferies have to do with me buying Freda's land? If I remember correctly, he wants it for himself."

"True, but you and I both know he isn't going to get it."

"Excuse me," Bonnie said. "I need to check on Freda."

Kayla and Warren were standing in front of the stairway, blocking the hallway.

"Sorry, Bonnie. Warren and I will be in the attic if you need us." Kayla tugged at Warren again. "Come on, Honey."

"Kayla, I swear you're enough to drive a man crazy. Please, try to talk in complete sentences and tell me what you meant by me having the land without paying for it. It's not fair to your family. They deserve something from Freda's inheritance."

"Upstairs, Warren. I have an idea."

"Apparently. Would you mind clueing me in on this?"

"All in good time, Dear. All in good time."

"Kayla, you're a tease." Slowly, they walked up the stairs with Kayla in the lead.

"I hope so. It's something we women are supposed to be good at." She winked.

"Trust me, Darlin', you leave the rest of the females in the dust. You don't need to perfect this trait."

"Why, thank you, Warren. I wasn't sure you noticed."

At the top of the attic stairs, she pulled the string dangling in front of her. Warren was a step below. She turned, not letting him pass. They were eye-to-eye. At six-foot-three, he was easily a head taller than she. Kayla draped her arms on his shoulders. "I've been thinking about my career, or lack thereof."

He reached up and pushed her hair from her eyes. "I know you gave up a lot to take care of Freda, Sweetheart. It's one of the things I love about you."

She forked her fingers through his dark chocolate hair. "And I was thinking about what Mack Jefferies said."

She felt him tense. "Which was?"

"He mentioned how more and more folks were commuting to the city and having an office at home."

"I'm sorry. I don't see what you're leading to."

Kayla groaned. "Okay, here's the deal. You want to stay on the land and be a farmer. The Lord has gifted you for it, and you're good at it."

Warren nodded his head in agreement.

"I, on the other hand, have felt led to go into the corporate world in the field of computer system analysis."

Warren nodded his head again.

"However, I can't begin my career until Gram. . ." Her voice caught in her throat. "Well, until after Gram passes away."

"Oh, Darling, I know it's tough, but hopefully she'll have more lucid moments like earlier tonight."

"I hope so, but I'm at peace with her passing, whenever it

might be. I don't need to hold on to her anymore. I truly have given her over to God. I trust Him with her life, and I'm leaving it up to Him to determine what kind of life she'll have on this earth."

"I'm glad, Kayla. But I'm still having a hard time following the connection."

Kayla blew an exasperated breath that teased her bangs. "Men," she huffed. "What I'm saying, Warren, is that I love you. I want to marry you, and I think I found a way to still have my career and marry you."

eighteen

Warren grasped the railing. Her words were so startling, he nearly fell backward. "You want to marry me?"

"Yeah, Cowboy. I want to marry you. And believe it or not, I want to be a farmer's wife."

"Yee-haw!" He bounced up the last step and lifted Kayla in his arms, twirling her around. "Are you certain? It's a hard life. We work from sunup to sundown."

"I think I'm well aware of your working hours." She winked.

Warren's heart raced. God was fulfilling his prayers. "Kayla, you've made me the happiest man on this earth."

"Then you accept my proposal?" She wiggled her eyebrows.

"Oh, yeah, on one condition."

"What?"

Did he dare risk her fragile proposal for their lives? "I want children, Kayla. Lots of them. I don't want my children growing up alone. My problem is, how will you work in the city and be able to take care of the kids?"

"Lots of children?" Her head jerked back. "Just how many are you thinking?"

"Five or six, whatever."

"I like the idea of two."

"We'll compromise and have four." Warren held her tighter. "Seriously, though, what about your career and children?"

"Can we deal with that when the time comes? I'm all for putting my children in their proper order of priorities."

"Proper order?" *Does she departmentalize everything?* he wondered.

"You know, God first, husband second, children third, career or anything after that, in their order of importance."

"So, you've thought this all out, have you?" he teased.

"Actually, I prayed it out," she countered. "So, will you marry me?" She kneaded her fingers on his shoulders and behind his neck.

"Isn't the man supposed to ask?" He had wanted to propose for weeks, but he thought she hadn't been ready. Now that she was, she just leapt ahead of him.

"Perhaps." She winked. "But before we go too far with our plans, we need to find those original documents. If I understood what Gram was saying, she's suggesting that she and Gramps controlled the water rights for the farmers." Kayla walked to the section of the attic they hadn't yet searched and reached into an old box.

Warren knew there was a manmade dam on the lake, and that the farmers each had a canal that fed off the lake, but he'd never thought any more about it. "Do you think Jefferies wants Freda's property so he can control the water?"

"He's got mighty big plans. He mentioned turning Gram's farm into the municipal area, with a school, town hall. . .you know, the works. I bet he figured it out from the town records. Obviously, Gram's not being taxed for the land under the lake. But I don't see how the town didn't just take the property. Don't they just do that?"

Warren leaned down and pulled up a wooden crate. "I bet that when they were organizing the town, it was just a bunch of farmers. And knowing that some towns charged for water, they probably figured they needed to control the water."

"It's certainly different. What I don't understand is why Gram never told anyone before now. Shouldn't she have told the family years ago?"

"Maybe she was afraid after seeing her son die so young,

and knowing that his son wasn't interested in farming. Maybe she just felt it best that no one knew."

"I guess." Kayla closed the box she'd been searching. Placing her hands upon her hips, she scanned the rest of the attic. "We're missing something. This shouldn't be this difficult."

"It does seem odd that we have to hunt for important documents. And she did say they were in the bank." Warren dusted his hands on his jeans. "What are you thinking, Darling?"

"I'm not sure. But Freda and Ed bought this place just before the Depression. We don't know when the lake was flooded or the canals made. And what I recall from history about folks who lived through the Depression, they had a genuine lack of trust for banks."

"Yeah, but the laws governing financial institutions changed, and Freda certainly used banks."

"True." Kayla sat on an old sofa. "But her safe-deposit box at the bank was something she did, not something Gramps did. He died when he was in his midforties. Which was around the late forties, early fifties."

Warren took a seat beside her. "Go on. I think I'm following you."

"So if these documents weren't in Gram's safe-deposit box, could they be in Gramps'?"

"I thought you just said he didn't have one. Now you've lost me, Girl."

"Come on. I think I know where it is." Kayla jumped up and flew down the stairs.

Warren scurried behind, turning off the light and shutting the door. When he rounded the stairs on the second floor to head down to the first floor, he saw her outside the house, running to the barn. "Where is she going?" he muttered.

❧

"It's got to be here. Gramps probably didn't trust the banks."

She gasped for breath.

"Kayla," Warren called.

"In the barn," she hollered. In the back of the barn, there was a small area with a workbench. It was there that her grandfather Max had done his woodworking.

"Kayla?"

The tall dark silhouette of Warren against a backdrop of gorgeous sunset caused her heart to flip-flop. Boy, had she ever fallen head over heels for that man. "Back here, Honey."

"Do you mind telling a fella what's gotten into that pretty little head of yours?"

"Sorry. This is where my grandfather Max used to work. While my grandpa Max farmed, his real love was working with wood. Anyway, before him, he used to tell me, this was his daddy's office."

Warren reached out and put his hand on her shoulder. His soothing touch helped her to calm down. "Anyway, I remember there used to be an old cast-iron box in here. Grandpa Max said that these were the kind of boxes used on stagecoaches in the Old West. The thing weighed a ton. But as a kid, I used to picture it sitting on the floor of the stagecoach beside the driver."

"A strongbox. Yeah, we have a couple, too."

"Exactly. And what were those things called?" She toyed with his collar—and his heart, she hoped.

"Sorry, I've always known them as strongboxes."

"Once Gramps called it 'the bank.' "

Kayla watched as Warren's eyes lit with excitement. "Hey, Watson, I think you've got it."

"Yeah, if we can find the strongbox." The two scoured the work area, opening cabinets, moving old boards leaning against the outer walls. Nothing.

Dusty, tired, and frustrated, she sat on an old bale of hay. "I can't believe it's not here. When I was real little, Grandpa would slide it over so I could stand on it."

"It's probably just been put somewhere else."

She knew it couldn't have gone far. Gram didn't sell anything. Freda still had piles of every *National Geographic* magazine she'd ever received. "So where is it?"

"My guess is as good as yours. But I'm sure it will turn up. Other than your father wanting to see the paperwork, I don't see any urgency for the document."

"I suppose, now that Gram's clarified the water deal. Remind me, I need to call my dad about that."

"Sure."

But something made the fine hairs on her neck stand up. She knew she needed to find that documentation and needed it soon. "Oh, no."

"What?" He pulled a strand of hay from her hair.

"You don't suppose the person who broke in already found it?"

"I suppose it's always possible, but that assumes they knew what they were looking for. And until these past few hours, no one knew. And we still aren't sure."

"There have to be other records. If it was an agreement with my great-grandfather and the other farmers, the others would have the records, too, wouldn't they?"

"Except there aren't too many of the original farmers in the area. My family, yours, the old Garret place. . . As you know, the Richmonds sold a couple years back to Jefferies."

"Do you have your cell phone?"

"Yes." Warren pulled it out of his pants pocket.

"Call your father. Ask him if he has an old agreement."

"Sure."

"I'll run into the house and call the Garrets."

"Okay."

Kayla found Bonnie at the dining room table, writing in the notebook Jean had said would be used to keep records. "Hi."

"Glad you came back. I'm just about ready to leave. Do you have any questions about taking care of Freda through the night?" Bonnie asked with pen in hand.

"No, she'll sleep most of the night, and with the flowing air mattress I don't need to keep turning her, right?"

"Right, she'll be fine. Jean will be back first thing in the morning."

"Thanks. I appreciate you ladies helping out."

Bonnie smiled. "Not a problem. It's what we're paid to do."

Kayla grabbed the phone book and thumbed through the Garrets. There had to be a dozen of them. "Which one?"

"Huh?" asked Bonnie, looking up.

"Sorry, I was talking with myself. Just trying to figure out which Garret is the older one."

"That would be Jasper. Wry old coot. I took care of him last summer."

"Thanks." Kayla's fingers trailed down the Js. "Got it." She punched in the numbers.

"Hello," an elderly male voice answered after six rings.

"Hi, Mr. Garret. I'm Freda's great-granddaughter, Kayla Brown."

"Well, I'll be. How's Freda? Heard she was having some trouble with her memory."

"She's doing pretty good. She developed Alzheimer's."

"Such a shame. She's got spunk. I always loved that about her."

"Thanks. The reason I'm calling is because of Gram's illness. We're having a hard time finding some of the old papers she said were around here. I was wondering if you might have a copy of an agreement between my great-grandfather Ed and yourself?"

"Sure do. It's with all my legal papers in my safe-deposit box. What do you need?"

"Well, we can't find Gram's copies of those, and with her trouble remembering things, we were hoping to get everything in order."

"Ed wasn't one for keeping things in the bank. Not after the stock market crashed. He tended to keep things close to him."

"That's what I was figuring, but I haven't found the papers yet."

"I'm sure they're around. But if you need a copy of mine, I can have a set made. Don't know what good it is. Just an agreement that the water is free for all of us to use. Most of the lake was built up on Ed's property, so we all decided he'd have the control of the water. But Ed felt it necessary to draw up the papers saying that as long as he or his descendants owned the land, the water would always be free to the five of us. Course, Richmond's grandson sold the farm to that contractor. You'd think that man would be happy with that complex. He's been wanting to buy my place, too."

"Ours, too," Kayla offered.

Jasper whistled. "Not selling, are you?"

"Nope, we're going to keep it in the family." Kayla smiled at Warren as he walked in.

"I'll sleep easy at night knowing that. Thanks. Don't think I could afford to pay for water. I get most I need off my own land, but what comes from the lake I use to feed the few head of cattle I raise."

"Well, as long as the land's in our family, you won't be having to worry about the water."

Kayla made her salutations and hung up the phone. "Jasper Garret has a copy of Ed's agreement about the water."

"Great. My father didn't know about the arrangement, but he went through some of the old files in the safe and found an agreement with his grandfather and your great-grandfather. So, when someone sold their property they must have given Mack Jefferies the copy of the agreement. Perhaps, as Dad says, there's a line in there that the rights are only good to pass down through the family lines. If it's sold, the new owner would need to make new arrangements."

"Interesting. Tell me, Warren, did Mack Jefferies pump water in from town or from the lake for that development?"

"I don't know. But Bill Masterson, the officer that came by the other day, bought one of those houses. Let's call him and ask."

Warren placed a call to the sheriff's office. After a few words with Bill, he hung up the phone. "Interesting."

"What?"

"Seems Bill and the others are paying Jefferies for the water purification and use."

"Oh, really?"

"Yeah, Bill and the sheriff are on their way over. I think you better call your father."

Kayla nodded and placed a call. It was short and sweet. "Dad says he thought something like that would be in the paperwork. He suggests we find Gramps's bank soon. He'll have his lawyer contact your father and Jasper for copies of their agreements, and he'll try and connect with Joe Richmond."

"The plot does thicken." Warren pulled her into his arms. "So, did you tell your father you asked me to marry you?"

Kayla giggled. "No. He'll want you to ask permission to ask for my hand. He's kind of old-fashioned that way."

"I see. So we're not really engaged yet?"

She wrapped her arms around his waist. "Oh, trust me, Cowboy, we're engaged."

Freda screamed.

nineteen

"Gram!" Kayla flew down the hall to Freda's bedroom. When she arrived, Freda was thrashing in her bed. A nightmare? Kayla sat on the bed beside her.

Warren stood at the foot of the bed.

"Gram, it's me, Kayla." She forked her grandmother's gray hair with her fingers and brushed the tossed strands off her face. "You're having a bad dream. Everything's all right."

Warren worked himself between the wall and other side of the bed.

Freda's eyes opened; her pupils were fully dilated.

Warren leaned over the bed and tenderly embraced Freda's hand. "We're here, Freda. Everything is okay."

"They were chasing me," Freda whispered.

"It's okay, Gram. It was just a dream. It didn't happen." Kayla caressed her grandmother's forehead and kissed her on the cheek, biting back the bitter tears. *No, I'm going to trust the Lord and His design for Gram's life,* she told herself, deliberately fortifying her resolve.

"Be careful. I think they're still here."

"I will, Gram. But Warren and I will watch out for you."

A loud knock on the front door made Kayla jump. Gram's scream had rattled her, even though the fright had only been a dream, a part of the nightmares that were a part of the delusions. *But still, a knock on the door shouldn't have made me jump,* she chastised herself.

"I'll get it. It's probably Bill and the sheriff," Warren spoke from the other side of the bed.

"Tell the police to find those bad men," Freda called out.

"I will." Warren smiled, then groaned, "Ouch."

"What's the matter?"

"I banged my toe on the corner of the bed." He looked down at his feet. "Hard, too. Looks like I busted the leg of the bed."

"Oh, no, that's been broke for years."

Warren nodded and hobbled toward the front door.

"Can you go back to sleep, Gram?"

"Is Max here?" Freda's eyes were focusing again. She looked less fearful than moments before when Kayla had entered the room.

"No, Gram. He's not here tonight."

"Oh. Doesn't that boy know when to come home? It's late."

Kayla chuckled to herself. She could see her grandpa Max giving his parents quite a time when he was a teen. "Yeah, he'll be here soon."

"All right." Freda settled back under the covers.

Kayla kissed her forehead and tucked the covers around her. She could hear the men talking in the front room and wanted to be a part of it. On the other hand, she needed to wait for a moment until Freda went back to sleep. She eased herself off the bed and worked her way to the far end to put the foot-board back in place. *I need to glue that in for her,* she thought. Freda's calm face reassured her she could leave, so she tucked the bed leg back in place and headed for the front room.

"Hello, Ms. Brown. Warren's been telling us some pretty interesting information." Sheriff Duffy stood about the same height as Warren, but he was broader in the shoulders and had that middle-aged paunch most men seem to get with the passing of time. Bill seemed out of place without his blue uniform.

"We thought so." Kayla sat beside Warren on the couch.

"So your father and Jasper have their original copies?" the sheriff asked Warren.

"Yes, Sir. And we're certain Ed's copy is here. We just haven't found it yet."

"Be good to have it. Who's the fifth farmer?"

Kayla looked at Warren. "Obviously, Joe Richmond was the fourth, but who else has a farm that connects with the canals from the lake?"

"Daniels. Tim Daniels's dad. But they're not the original family. Who'd he buy the land from?" Warren asked Sheriff Duffy.

"Bill, wasn't that Curt Riley's place before Jim Daniels bought it?"

"I believe so. But if what they say is true, Jim Daniels needed to make an arrangement with Freda after he bought the place, too," Bill recalled.

"Which means he'd have the original document, plus a new one from Freda." The sheriff sat back in Gram's favorite chair and rubbed his chin.

"Sheriff, if Mack Jefferies was supposed to make arrangements with my grandmother, he would have had to have done it before I started living here. Because I know he never made arrangements with her while I was here. But if he didn't, wouldn't there be a problem with him using the water and charging for it?"

"Oh, yeah, there would be a mighty big problem. Fact is, for the amount of houses he's building, that lake won't support the farms and the houses," Bill piped in. "Ever since the transformer blew, we've seen more and more cases of Jefferies cutting corners on construction costs. The original plans called for him digging some wells and eventually piping in water from the town."

Kayla thought about the ramifications to Mack Jefferies and his grand plans. Not to mention, she might have the right to sue him for the amount he'd been charging the residents.

She didn't like the idea of lawsuits, but she also didn't like Mack Jefferies and his kind of business.

"I'll pull up the building permit and zoning files, and look into the plans Jefferies filed with the town. I'll make certain he's doing everything he's supposed to be doing. But, Ms. Brown, you'll need to find those papers. We can prove there was an agreement by the two men who still have them, but control of the lake and the water rights will remain in limbo until you find those papers."

"I understand, Sheriff. I'm sure we'll find them soon."

Sheriff Duffy cleared his throat. "Also, I'm afraid we can't tell you who broke into the house. The prints we found that weren't yours, your grandmother's, or Warren's couldn't be identified."

Then who broke in?

"I suspect it's only kids and someone who's never been in trouble before. . .thus the reason for the lack of prints."

"I still have a hard time believing someone would break in when the doors are always unlocked." Kayla slid over toward Warren. He placed his hand around her shoulder.

"Another reason why we're pretty sure it was kids. If the kids were smart enough, they would have tried the doors. With all the new folks that have moved in over at the development, they aren't too far from your place. So a couple kids with nothing to do could have been a little too curious."

Kayla let out a breath. "You're probably right, but I'd love to catch them and throttle them."

Bill chuckled. "Leave the throttling to us. We can scare a few years off of them and hopefully keep them from getting into the wrong crowd."

Kayla nodded. He was probably right, but she couldn't deny the fact that she'd love to give them the "what for" herself.

"Well, it's late, and we need to be going. Thanks for letting us know about the water agreements. We'll keep in touch." Sheriff Duffy got up, and his holster clapped the side of his thigh. They all shook hands, and the officers quietly departed.

"What a day." Kayla leaned into Warren's arms.

"Yeah, what a day." Warren grinned.

❧

A week later, Warren waved good-bye to Kayla as he picked up his toolbox. "See you later."

Today he was watching Freda while Kayla did some errands. Jean and Bonnie had quickly become a part of everyone's lives over the past week, but today Jean had a personal appointment, and Bonnie was coming in two hours late. Warren had volunteered to take care of Freda.

All week, he'd been wanting to repair the broken leg to Freda's bed. All week, he'd been so busy he hadn't had a chance. Watching Freda would allow him the time and opportunity to get the job done.

He stepped into Freda's room and glanced quickly at the bed. The bed was typical of the Depression era: functional working furniture, nothing fancy. The leg was a simple tapered rectangle, narrowing with a slight curve at the foot.

Retreating back to the living room, he asked, "How's my favorite gal today?"

Freda didn't answer. Instead, she sat looking off into space. Warren glanced over in the general direction she was looking, but he couldn't find anything to hold her attention.

He checked her safety belt, tapped her lightly on the top of her hand, and gave her a kiss. "I'm going to run to the barn and get some shunts to brace the bed leg. I'll be right back."

Warren left her in the living room and headed toward the kitchen. In the doorway, he turned to see if she was watching him. Nothing, no response. She was still staring at the same corner of the wall. *You know, Lord, it's hard to see her like this.*

Warren jogged at a healthy pace to the barn. He didn't want to leave her alone for long. *She was safe for now, but there was no telling when she'd snap out of this phase,* he reminded himself.

Inside the barn, he looked for some slender pieces of wood to set the clamps against so he wouldn't mar the leg. A couple small strips of fir, and he was all set. He glanced around the barn, searching every nook and cranny. Kayla and he had been through every inch of this barn, but they'd never recovered the strongbox. Still not seeing it, he pulled himself back to the house.

Freda's gaze had shifted and was piercing through the living room into the kitchen when Warren stepped through. "So, she is aware to some extent that I'm here," he mumbled.

He stepped up behind Freda and grabbed the wheelchair handles. "Come on, Freda, we've got a bed to repair." There was barely enough room for the wheelchair in the bedroom, but Warren didn't want to leave her alone staring at nothing.

He went back into the living room and retrieved his toolbox. Pulling out the epoxy, clamps, and tile on which to mix the two substances together, he laid out what he needed. Getting down on his knees, he was about to go down on all fours, when he remembered he needed to brace the bed with something.

"Be right back, Freda. I need a cement block."

Freda nodded.

"That's my girl. We're making progress." He kissed the top of her head and headed out back, where he pulled a concrete block from Kayla's flower garden. Dusting off the dirt, he hauled it to Freda's room.

He got down on his hands and knees and slid the block under the bed a few inches from the leg.

The block stopped.

"What on earth?" Warren got down lower and peered under the bed. A dark box appeared to already be holding up the corner of the bed.

"Of course. Kayla said it had been broken for years." Warren pushed the concrete block away from the bed and lifted the corner slightly, pulling off the leg. The wood was splintered but able to be glued.

He leaned lower and looked at the black box holding up the bed. "Wonder what it is?" He reached back and felt the coolness of metal.

Metal?

Iron?

"The strongbox. No way." He stood up and lifted the corner of the bed and saw that it definitely was the strongbox.

"Freda, you won't believe how long we've been looking for this." Warren fished for the concrete block and pushed it under the bed, then he reached for the cast-iron handle on the side of the strongbox to pull it out.

"My bank," Freda announced.

"Yeah, I kinda figured that." Warren grinned. The cast-iron box weighed a ton. But the padlock on it shouted, *Close, but not quite there yet!*

He set the strongbox aside and continued his chore of fixing the bed leg. *She's been sleeping on it all this time, Lord. Amazing.*

❧

"You found it?"

Kayla had returned home a couple hours later. Just enough time for Warren to finish repairing the bed and set Freda down in it for her afternoon nap, then search the desk, kitchen drawers, and anyplace else he could think of to try and find the key to "the bank."

"Yep, but we can't open it. I can get a hacksaw and cut

through the lock, but that will take hours. I've looked through the desk, the kitchen drawers—everywhere I could think of for the key—no luck. I even tried a few keys, but nothing's worked so far."

Kayla tapped her delicate finger to her lips. The red nail polish was the perfect accent to her rose print dress. Her eyes widened. "I bet I know."

"Where?"

"Her jewelry box."

"Her jewelry box? You're kidding, right?"

"No, we women tend to put important things in jewelry boxes."

"Yeah, like jewelry—but not keys."

"Trust me, Cowboy, more than jewelry gets put in a lady's jewelry box."

He'd trust her, but he might just take a peek at his mother's to see if this was a normal trend.

Kayla slipped into Freda's room without a sound and returned looking like she'd swallowed a canary, waving a brass key in front of her face. "You knew it was there?"

"Just a hunch," she winked.

Warren raked his hair back with his fingers and wondered what else women kept in their jewelry boxes.

Kayla slipped the key into the padlock. "Bingo," she said as she turned the key and the lock popped open.

twenty

Kayla's heart pounded with anticipation. The first thing to catch her attention was a stack of letters tied with a pink ribbon. She removed the well-worn ribbon and read for a moment.

"These are letters to Gram from a variety of folks." She shuffled through the pile down toward the bottom. Her hand faltered. "Oh, my."

Warren slid an arm around her.

"This is a letter I wrote as a child. I remember giving my parents a fit because they said I had to write it." A salty tear stung her eyelids. She swallowed hard and put the letters aside.

Warren reached in and pulled out an old portfolio envelope, then handed it to Kayla. She fished it open and found old news clippings. Each clipping was about one of Freda's children, grandchildren, and, most recently, her great-grandchildren. It even included Freda's husband's obituary, along with her son Max's. "She saved the strangest things."

"Oh, I don't know. Seems to me each article made her proud, or, in the case of the obituaries, sad. One thing is certain, she loved her family."

"Yeah." Kayla reached into the strongbox and pulled out the next item. It was the documentation of a loan Freda had taken out shortly after Ed's death. She moved farther down the stack of important papers, each item getting darker due to the aging of time. On the bottom she discovered another portfolio envelope. Her hands shook as she reached for the single remaining item. "This has to be it; it's the last item."

"I hope so. Do you want me to open it?" Warren asked, massaging her shoulder.

"No, I'm okay. Just nervous that after all this searching it's not even in the strongbox."

"It'll be all right, Kayla. The Lord will take care of us."

"I know, but I've grown to dislike Mack Jefferies and his get-rich plans on the backs of others."

"He'll be stopped. The sheriff, not to mention the town, won't let him get away with code violations. He'll be fixing up his development or paying some large fees so that others can do the work."

"I suppose, but he cheated Gram, too. Took advantage of her diminished mental abilities."

"I know, Darling, but give it to God. Otherwise, we'll get eaten up with anger."

Kayla let out a deep breath. "You're right, Warren." She untied the old ribbon and pulled out the first document. "The original deed to the property."

"All right, Freda."

Anxiously, she reached in for the next item: an aged brown envelope that simply said "Agreement" on the outside. Carefully, she opened the brittle pages. "Yes, this is it."

"Hallelujah, thank You, Lord," Warren praised.

"Amen." Kayla quickly scanned the letter. In her grandfather's own handwriting, he had spelled out how he'd donated the land to build a reservoir to help feed the five farms. He stated who the five were and the agreement that was reached between them, dated and signed by all five men.

"What else is in the portfolio?" Warren asked.

Kayla pulled out an old legal parchment. "Look, Warren, Grandpa Ed brought the agreement to a lawyer and had it legally spelled out. No one is entitled to that water except the farmers and their families."

"Interesting." Warren captured the document and read on further. Chuckling, he added, "Appears your great-grandfather was a very wise man. Since the land belonged to him, there was a provision in the agreement that, should the lands cease to be farmlands, he had the right to drain the reservoir and make use of those 200 acres, him or his descendants." Warren put the document down on the table. "Can you imagine how rich that land would be under that water? Because farmers use the water to feed their livestock, there's never been any motorized boats on the lake. At least, not as far back as I can remember."

"But what does this mean for Gram, for Mack Jefferies?" Kayla prodded.

"It means, Darling, Mack Jefferies's troubles just got worse." Warren stepped over to the phone and punched in a call. "Sheriff Duffy, please."

Kayla scanned the documents while she half-listened to Warren's phone conversation. Primarily, she was interested in the fragments of Freda's life scattered across the table. All of the items were treasured moments of time. She reached for the letter she'd written when she was eight.

Dear Grandma,
   I want to thank you for your present. I like it vary much. I wish you were here four Christmas. Dad says you're with our cousins and we have to share. I love you, Gram.

                                                    Love,
                                                    Kayla

Kayla couldn't hold back the lump in her throat. She'd genuinely meant the words at the time, but to see them now all these years later, and to see the place of importance it held for

Freda, she felt she should have written more letters or called her more often when she was at college.

≈

Warren returned the phone to its cradle. Seeing tears in Kayla's eyes, he protectively wrapped her in his arms. "There's pain in grief, Darling, but it's good for the soul."

"I just should have done more."

"You've done quite a bit, and are still doing it," he reminded her as he nuzzled his nose in her hair.

"I know, but she doesn't know me now. I meant I should have sent her more letters when I was a kid, called her more, visited her more. You know?"

"Ah, but do you think Freda didn't realize you were just like she was when she was a young girl? Life brings perspective." Warren groaned. "I swore I'd never say those words."

"Huh?"

" 'Life brings perspective.' My folks say that all the time. Drove me crazy when I was a teen. Now, I see things differently, at least enough to know my folks had that right. But what I meant is, Freda's lived a very rich life. She's a wise woman, Kayla. She knows her children, grandchildren, and even great-grandchildren needed to live their lives. I'm sure she would have loved more visits, but she's always been an extremely practical woman. I don't think she went around moaning that she never saw her family."

"You're right. I guess I'm just letting guilt take over."

"I've heard it said that guilt is a part of the grieving process, and while Freda's still alive and kicking—whom we should be checking on, by the way—she's no longer who she once was, and you're grieving."

"I guess you're right. I do need to check on Gram. Bonnie should be here soon."

"Great. Sheriff Duffy wants to see the original documents

to make copies of them. He also said we needed to get them in the hands of your father's attorneys."

"Agreed. Why don't you run them to the sheriff? I'll call Dad after I take care of Gram."

"Sounds good." Warren reached for his Stetson where it sat flipped upside down on the table. He placed it on his head and released Kayla after stealing a brief kiss.

He was glad to have the opportunity to go to town. The ring he'd ordered had come in and was sitting at the post office waiting for his signature. Kayla didn't know, but he had special plans for her tonight. Bonnie's coming in late was actually his idea.

"See you later, Darlin'."

Kayla grinned and retreated to the back bedroom.

Lord, I love that woman. Thank You for her tender heart. He slipped into the cab of his truck as he prayed.

❧

The sheriff perused the documents and immediately made copies of them. The U.S. Postal Service was reliable, but original copies weren't worth the risk.

Warren said good-bye, then buzzed over to the post office and signed for his package. After a few more stops, he went to Jackson's Supplies.

As he worked his way through the aisles, he looked up to find Brian Jackson standing with his hands on his hips and legs parted slightly, blocking the end of the aisle.

"I've got a bone to pick with you," Brian called out.

Warren quelled his temper. He needed victory over his feelings of jealousy and anger with this man. "What's up, Brian?"

"Word is, you and Kayla Brown are engaged." Brian scowled.

"Word is correct."

Brian's posture shifted. "Seriously, Man, are you really going to marry Kayla?"

"Yes."

"I don't get it. I could have offered her so much. Guess I didn't have a chance with you always being over there."

"Possibly. Brian, I know you're a Christian—so don't you believe in God directing folks with their choices for a spouse?"

Brian shuffled his feet.

Warren continued. "Brian, I prayed a long time and waited what seemed an eternity for my spouse. And when I became attracted to Kayla, I knew with every ounce of my being she was the one. Although it took her quite a bit longer to realize it, too. Which, of course, caused me to wonder if I was reading God correctly or not. Don't you want the best one God has designed for you?"

"I suppose. I just figured she was attractive, so we'd make a handsome couple. She's nice to talk with, figured it would work out."

"What did God say?" Warren pushed.

"Didn't ask Him."

"Hmm, the biggest decision a man's going to make in his entire life, and you choose not to ask God?"

"Kinda stupid, right?" Brian grinned, tossing his head from side to side.

"Right."

"I'm probably branching out into a new business, and that will be time-consuming for a while. I won't have much time for a wife."

"What's the new business?" Warren asked.

"I've been looking to become a part owner of Mack Jefferies Construction."

"Uh, Brian, I'd really pray about that decision."

Brian lifted his right eyebrow. "Look, Warren, I know you're not interested in selling your land for development, but Mack's got some great plans. And his numbers look really impressive."

"It's not the farming and development that bothers me. There are other issues. Just pray, Brian. I can't say anything else."

Brian rubbed his chin. "This doesn't have anything to do with his pushing Kayla to sell Freda's property and him filing for an incompetency hearing on Freda, does it?"

"He's doing what?"

"You hadn't heard?"

"No, and apparently, neither has Kayla. What's going on?"

"Mack figures that once the family is forced to take away Freda's control of the property, they'll sell it to him just to pay the cost of the nursing home."

Warren couldn't believe the lengths the man was willing to go to get Freda's land. On the other hand, he had a lot at stake. If he were able to purchase the land, he'd own the land under the water, and the water rights would be in his control. "Seems to me old Mack doesn't have a clue what's in Freda's will. If the family sells the land, they have to sell it to a farmer. Plus, she's stipulated who she wants to purchase the land and for how much."

"Why would she do that?"

"I can't guess the reasons why, but I do know folks have been asking her and her husband to sell that property for fifty years. The answer's always been no, and always will be as long as she's alive."

"But she's crazy. Is this a new will?"

Warren knew where Brian was headed. "No, and it's perfectly legal. She wrote it years before she developed Alzheimer's. And by the way, Brian, Alzheimer's is a disease affecting the arteries in the brain. It has nothing to do with psychosis."

"Still, she doesn't know anything," Brian amended. "I didn't mean anything by it. I just know she's crazy, doesn't know who she is, can't hold a conversation with folks. You know."

"Yeah, I know." Warren wasn't going to spend the day arguing Freda's problems. And with what he had just learned, he thought it might be best to pay Mr. Mack Jefferies a little visit. "I've got to run. I'd be happy to talk with you more about Freda's condition at another time."

It didn't take long for Warren to arrive at Mack Jefferies's trailer on the site of his newest development. With determined steps, he marched up to Mack's door and knocked.

"Come in."

"Help me, Lord," Warren whispered as he turned the handle.

twenty-one

Warren marveled at how pale Mack Jefferies's face appeared as he sank farther back in his leather office chair. How quickly his expression had changed when he informed Mack Jefferies that his plans wouldn't succeed. "So, you see, you cannot contest the will, nor would there be any point in a competency hearing."

For the past ten minutes, Warren had shared the contents of Freda's will regarding the land. He'd seen a glimmer of hope in Mack's eyes when he'd heard that a member of the family would inherit the land if they chose to farm it. But when Warren laid out that only a farmer could purchase it, and the price was designated, he'd slumped back.

"So, why are you bringing this to my attention?" Mack regained his poker face.

"Because you and I both know what you are up to, and it's going to stop."

"You have no idea what I'm up to," Mack hissed.

Warren placed his hands palm down on Mack's desk and leaned toward him just a bit. "Oh, I reckon I have a pretty good idea. Cheating people out of what's rightfully theirs, building substandard homes, code violations, and the list could go on."

Mack's poker face slipped. "Everything is explainable. Besides, the power company is fixing their mistake and putting in the right transformer."

"The transformer is the least of your worries. You forget something, Mack. My grandfather purchased the land around the same time as Ed Brown did. There were five farmers who put together an interesting water co-op. Three families are still in control of their original rights. The fourth farmer has an updated copy of his rights. You, Sir, purchased the fifth farm, and you violated those rights. Knowing Freda's diminished mental capacity, you figured it wouldn't matter. But you were wrong. Dead wrong.

"We are prepared, and legal actions are already in the works. I suggest you get your act together, and get it together fast, or you'll be facing some serious fines and possible jail time."

"You ain't got nothing but an old letter from a man who's been dead for nearly fifty years." Mack's face reddened and his eyes bulged.

"Oh, we've got more than the letters, Mack."

The blood drained from Mack's face, leaving a gray pallor to it. "You're bluffing, Robinson."

"Our lawyers will be in touch." Warren stood and walked toward the door. "Oh, one more thing. I never bluff."

Settled in the cab of his truck, he paused for a moment. "Thanks, Lord, for not letting me lose my temper in there." Warren turned on the engine and drove toward Tim Daniels's farm. He'd been concerned from the moment he heard Tim was delivering envelopes for Mack.

❧

Jim Daniels was happy to give Warren a copy of his agreement with Freda so he could send everything to Charles Brown's attorney. Tim walked into the living room after the men's business was finished.

"Hey, Warren, thought that was your truck. Got some more work for me?"

Warren chuckled. "Afraid not, Sport. However, I wanted to speak with you and your dad about you not doing any more work for Mack Jefferies."

"Not a problem. I already quit. Fact is, after Dad spoke with Sheriff Duffy, it was a done deal." Tim sat on the rocking chair across from Warren.

Jim piped in. "Once you called about the water rights, I spoke with Tim about these 'packages' he's been delivering. Sheriff was mighty interested in those, too. Especially when they went to a couple of key members of the town council."

"Some of them wouldn't take the envelopes. Dad thinks it was bribe money. Don't know myself, I never opened up the envelopes. But the shape would be right, I suppose."

"I see, and Sheriff Duffy knows about this?"

"Yep. He knows about every person and when I made the deliveries. I had to keep a record in order for Mack Jefferies to pay me at the end of each week."

Warren chuckled. "I think Mr. Jefferies will be having quite a few headaches in the near future."

"Oh, forgot to tell you. I was asking around about Freda's house and the possible break-ins." Tim sat forward in his chair. "It was a couple of the new boys. Said it was a double-dare thing. They didn't take anything. . .just being stupid."

Warren rose from the sofa. "Tell them to come see me at Kayla's tomorrow around dinnertime. They can apologize to her." He'd also have a list of chores for the boys to help them repent and clear their consciences.

❧

After a quick shower and a change of clothes, he had called Kayla and told her to be ready to go out to dinner. Now he parked the truck and turned off the engine. Would she be ready? He worried his lower lip, then clasped the bouquet of flowers he'd purchased while in town as he slipped out of the cab. At the front door, he knocked, buffing the toes of his boots on the back of his pant legs.

"Hey, Cowboy, when did you start knocking?" Kayla beamed. Her auburn hair framed her beautiful face. Her green eyes sparkled.

"When a man comes a-callin,' it's proper to knock before stomping into the house." He held back his grin.

"And if you think I buy that, I've got some great swampland for sale."

"Hmm, speaking of swamplands. . ." He stepped into the house and was about to recount his trip into town when he reminded himself, *Tonight is for wooing, not business.* "Kayla, you're beautiful. You absolutely take my breath away."

"And apparently your mind. What were you going to say about swamplands?" Kayla placed her hands on her hips.

The dress she wore of emerald green and white lace accented her beauty. The hands on her hips let him know she meant business. He placed the bouquet on the table and pulled her into his embrace. "With you looking so wonderful, who wants to talk business? Let me greet you properly, my love."

❧

Kayla melted in Warren's arms, anticipating his sweet kiss. She reached up and entwined her arms around his neck. "Oh, Honey, I missed you today. I'm so glad you arranged for Bonnie to come in late. I'm really looking forward to going out with you."

"Me, too, Darlin'. Kayla, I need to ask you something."

In spite of the confidence in their budding relationship, Kayla stiffened slightly. They'd been so busy working for Freda, meeting her needs and the family's needs, they'd hardly had time for themselves. She wanted to marry him, or else she wouldn't have proposed, but she was still a little nervous. "Okay, shoot."

"Kayla, you're the most fascinating woman I've ever met. Your heart is pure gold when it comes to loving and helping others. You're more beautiful than any man could imagine, and I'm so honored that you've asked me to marry you. However. . ." She shifted in his arms slightly, waiting for the other shoe to drop. "Being a man, and a rather proud one sometimes, I was wondering if you'd do me the honor of agreeing to become my wife?"

Kayla's heart soared and a giggle surfaced. "Warren, my love, I can't think of anything else I want more. Yes—" She cut herself from babbling on and on by leaning into him and kissing him soundly on the lips.

He released her and stepped back slightly. "Well, in that case, I'd be mighty honored if you'd wear this ring as a symbol of our promises to each other. When the time is right, we'll marry."

"Warren," Kayla gasped. A gold ring with a teardrop emerald in a Tiffany setting sparkled as she held out her hand. He slipped it on. Her hands shook. "It's beautiful."

"Not as beautiful as the woman wearing it."

"Can I see?" Bonnie called out from the hallway. "I knew he was going to propose to you tonight."

Kayla giggled and held out her hand. Warren's grin filled his entire face.

"It's beautiful, and the emerald brings out the color of your eyes," Bonnie commented. "You did good, Warren."

Warren nodded.

"Is Gram still awake?"

"Yeah, I think she'd enjoy seeing you and hearing about your plans."

Kayla headed into Freda's room. "Hi, Gram," she yelled, loud enough for the folks across the lake to hear her. *Well, maybe not quite that loud.* Kayla grinned.

"Hi. Do I know you?"

"Yes, Gram, I'm Kayla, your great-granddaughter."

"Oh. Kayla's a pretty name. It was my mother's name. I have a granddaughter named Kayla. Do you know my granddaughter?"

epilogue

Seven months later

Freda held the blanket tighter. She gasped for air. Her lungs ached. "Oh, Lord, how much longer do I have to wait?"

"It's time, Freda. Come home."

Freda felt her last breath leave her. Her mind cleared. It had been ages since she could think straight. She could see the brightness of God's throne as she felt herself float toward heaven. "I'm going home."

She smiled. Kayla and Warren were in the living room making their wedding plans. She saw the farm and the land Ed had worked so hard to protect, the budding mustard tree beside the lake. But they paled to the glory that awaited her. She continued to rise. The light increased.

"Come, Freda. Welcome home."

RESCUE

*H*owever they communicate it, the friends you are about to make within this book are in peril—of body, heart, and soul. It may take a daring intervention—and some divine help—to get them out of their frightening situations.

Fasten your safety belt as you head into these four adventures. Life and love are at risk, but it's comforting to know that God, as always, is ultimately in control.

paperback, 352 pages, 5 ³/₁₆" x 8"

❤ ❤ ❤ ❤ ❤ ❤ ❤ ❤ ❤❤ ❤ ❤ ❤ ❤ ❤ ❤ ❤ ❤

❤ ❤ ❤ ❤ ❤ ❤ ❤ ❤ ❤❤ ❤ ❤ ❤ ❤ ❤ ❤ ❤ ❤